Lemon Chiffon Lies

The Drunken Pie Café Cozy Mysteries, Book Three

Diana DuMont

CHAPTER ONE

"We're sold out of lemon vodka pie again?" I asked in disbelief. The summery lemon pie had been one of the Drunken Pie Café's most popular flavors over the last several weeks, and I'd done my best to bake extra large batches every morning before opening for business. But no matter how many lemon vodka pies I baked, I couldn't keep up.

Not that I was complaining. Selling out of pie was a good problem to have. I had taken a leap of faith when I moved to Sunshine Springs to start my boozy pie café, but it appeared that my leap of faith was paying off. I'd made enough profits lately to pay all my bills on time, and even to start slowly rebuilding my savings account. Life was good.

"Sold out again," Ruby Phillips confirmed with a grin, flipping her strawberry blonde ponytail backward over her shoulder. I had hired Ruby last week, and I already didn't know how I had managed to survive running the Drunken Pie Café without her. Ruby had proven to be an efficient employee and a quick learner, and I caught myself thanking my lucky stars several times a day that my search for a part-time employee had ended with her.

The bell above the front door jingled, and Ruby and I both turned our attention toward the café's entrance. I smiled when I saw Scott Hughes, who worked as a package delivery man in Sunshine Springs. Scott had been one of my first friends in Sunshine Springs, and he was a good friend to have. Since he spent his days traveling around town delivering packages, he always knew the latest, juiciest gossip.

1

Today, he was carrying a small, shoebox-sized package, which he handed over to me with a grin.

"Online shopping again? Don't you think you have enough pairs of shoes already?"

I gave him a cross look. "Don't you think you should mind your own business?"

Scott let out a hearty laugh. "When have I ever minded my own business? You know me better than that."

I smiled. "True. Any good gossip to share today?"

Scott shook his head. "No. Things have been unbearably dull around here since you solved the Edgar Bates murder case. There's not even anyone cheating on their spouse, as far as I know. The most exciting thing I've heard all day is that the City Council decided to add a dog show to the fall festival this year."

I perked up with interest. "A dog show? Maybe I should enter Sprinkles."

My Dalmatian, Sprinkles, had become well-known around town. He was the only Dalmatian around, and in addition to his flashy, spotted coat, he was often sporting brightly colored toenails. My Grams, who often petsat for me while I was working at the café, liked to take Sprinkles to the salon with her and get his nails painted in neon shades. I had long since given up on trying to convince her that my boy dog didn't need to have his nails painted.

Scott rolled his eyes. "Like that dog needs any more attention than he already gets. Where is he now, anyway? With your Grams?"

I nodded, but before I could say anything else, Ruby piped in with her opinion.

"I think you should enter Sprinkles in the dog show. Why not? He's a beautiful dog, and I bet he'd win."

I grinned at Ruby, thankful for the show of support, but Scott scowled at her. He hadn't liked Ruby from day one, which surprised me somewhat. Usually, Scott got along with everyone. I suspected that his dislike of her had something to do with the fact that Ruby working at the café meant that my best friend, Molly, wasn't working here anymore. Molly had a fulltime job as the head librarian of the Sunshine Springs Public Library, but that hadn't stopped her from helping me out in the middle of the summer when my café was busy and I'd been desperate for any help I could get. Scott had enjoyed being able to pop in and talk to both Molly and me at the same time, and his talking had often been borderline flirting. Molly and I both had no romantic interest in him, but that hadn't stopped him from trying.

"Well, anyway," Scott said flatly. "You have time to think about it. It's barely September, and the festival isn't until the end of October. It's hard to believe that fall will ever arrive, if you ask me. It's still unbearably hot out right now."

"I love the heat," Ruby declared brightly, earning her another scowl from Scott.

"I love the heat, too," I said. "It puts everyone in the mood for lemon pie."

"Sold out again?" Scott asked, looking over at the café's display case with a frown. "That's a shame. I was hoping to snag a piece."

"Sold out," I confirmed. "In fact, I'm going to have to go get more fresh lemons from my supplier in the next town over. I don't even have enough lemons left to bake another batch of pies tomorrow."

"You can go now, if you want," Ruby said. "I don't mind closing out the store for you."

I smiled at her gratefully. "If you're sure you don't mind? I know you haven't closed by yourself yet. Are you sure you won't be overwhelmed by all the closing duties?"

Ruby waved her hand dismissively. "I can handle it. It's not that complicated, and if I have questions I can always call you."

I nodded, feeling relieved. If I left to get the lemons now, I could probably make it back before the late afternoon tourist traffic got really bad. And Ruby was right: closing up the café wasn't all that complicated. I had been babying Ruby a bit because I wanted her to have a good experience as an employee and not feel overwhelmed. It had taken me so long to find an employee that I was terrified of Ruby being unhappy and quitting. But Ruby seemed eager to help, and I desperately needed her help.

As I reached back to start untying my apron strings, the bell above the front door jangled again. I turned to see Belinda Simmons waltzing in, bringing with her a cloud of citrusy-smelling perfume.

"Belinda!" Ruby squealed. "I was hoping you'd stop by today. How is the scavenger hunt for Tom going?"

I saw a scowl cross Scott's face once again, and I gave him a warning punch in the arm. In addition to Ruby, Belinda also made the very short list of people whom Scott didn't like.

Honestly, I couldn't blame Scott for not liking Belinda. Belinda had shamelessly cheated on her ex-husband with her current boyfriend, Tom. As a divorcée myself, I understood that sometimes marriages couldn't be saved, but that didn't mean I condoned cheating on a spouse. I agreed with Scott that Belinda should have ended things with her ex-husband before starting things with Tom.

But at the end of the day, it wasn't my business what Belinda did with her life. And because Belinda had become fast friends with Ruby, Belinda spent quite a bit of time at the Drunken Pie Café. This meant that Belinda bought quite a bit of pie from me, and I wasn't one to turn away a paying customer. Thankfully, Scott took my hint and smoothed his scowl into a smile, although he did turn his back on Belinda and Ruby.

"I should get going," he said. "I still have quite a few deliveries to make, and I promised Molly I'd go see a movie with her when she gets off work tonight."

I frowned slightly. "Why wasn't I invited?" Molly, Scott and I spent so much time together that a few of the townspeople had affectionately nicknamed us the three musketeers. I couldn't help feeling a bit miffed that the two of them had forgotten to include me in their plans to hang out, but Scott was shaking his head at me in an amused fashion.

"We did invite you. Don't you remember? You said you were too busy to waste two hours of your life watching the latest Hollywood drivel."

I blushed. Now that Scott said that, I realized he was right. I did remember being invited to see a movie with them, but I'd begged off because I was worried that Ruby wouldn't stick it out as an employee. Those fears had proven unfounded—Ruby was doing a fantastic job, and didn't show any signs of wanting to quit. But still, I probably was too busy to justify an evening at the movies. I needed to get more lemons, and I had a few new pie recipes I wanted to try out tonight. Even though I'd finally found a dependable employee, I was still playing catch up on quite a few things.

"Right," I said sheepishly. "I guess I did decline your invite. And I am quite busy tonight. But you two have fun."

Scott grinned. "We will. We'll gossip about you all night since you won't be there."

I groaned and punched his arm again. "You're a horrible friend," I teased. "But thankfully I don't think there's any interesting gossip about me at the moment."

"No, I don't think so. I don't think there's interesting gossip about anyone at the moment." Scott lowered his voice so that only I could hear him. "Even the gossip about Belinda and Tom has gotten old. No one's interested anymore in what she and Tom are doing. Well, no one but Ruby, that is."

I glanced over at Ruby and Belinda, who were giggling like schoolgirls. I had no doubt they were discussing whatever Belinda's latest over-the-top romantic surprise was for Tom. I winced as I thought of Belinda's poor ex-husband, Frank. For his sake, I was glad that the gossip mill was finally tiring of Belinda's and Tom's relationship. I was sure Frank must be tired of hearing about how in love Belinda was with her new boyfriend.

The bell above the door jangled again, and I looked up to see Grams walking in, with Sprinkles close on her heels.

"Grams!" I said in surprise. "I thought you had bridge club this afternoon."

"I did," Grams said with a dramatic sigh. "But Rose is sick, so it was postponed. I stopped by to see if you had any lemon vodka pie. This heat wave is awful, and I sure could use a good slice of lemon pie to cool down with."

Scott, whom I had to admit could be a perfect gentleman when he wanted to be, quickly rushed to grab Grams' arm and help her into a chair at one of the café's tables. "Lemon pie's all gone," he informed her sadly. "I was also hoping for a slice, but Izzy's sold out."

Grams shook her head at me, her neon green hair bouncing against her shoulders as she did. "You need to make more of that lemon pie. You're always selling out!"

Grams had a thing for bright colors, and frequently changed her hair from one shade of neon to another. She also wore the brightest outfits you could imagine. Today, she had on a bright orange blouse and neon green pants that matched her hair. She was a character, but she was the best grandmother I could have wanted. She stood by me even when the rest of the world wanted to beat me down. Thankfully, the rest of the world was leaving me alone at the moment. Life was good, and I decided to come around the front counter to sit by Grams for a few moments.

5

"We've still got strawberry moonshine pie," I said. "I know you like that one. And I've been trying to make more lemon pie, but I can't keep up. This heat wave has made all of my summer flavors quite popular, but the lemon most of all."

Grams sighed dramatically. "I guess I'll settle for strawberry moonshine pie."

I nodded and stood once more to get her the pie. "Do you want a piece?" I asked Scott over my shoulder. But Scott shook his head no.

"I really do need to get going. I don't want to be late for the movie with Molly tonight, and I still have quite a few deliveries to make. You ladies enjoy your pie."

As soon as Scott had left, Grams looked at me and raised an eyebrow. "What's going on with Scott and Molly?"

I didn't like the conspiratorial tone in her voice, so I raised an eyebrow right back at her. "What do you mean?"

"I mean that I've never seen Scott looking so giddy about going to see a movie with someone. And he wasn't flirting with you like he normally does. If I didn't know better, I'd think he and Molly are becoming an item."

"Oh, don't be ridiculous," I retorted. "Scott and Molly are just friends. They have been forever. And fine by me if he doesn't flirt with me anymore. I've been trying to get him to stop with that nonsense forever."

Even as I said these words, however, I couldn't help wondering if Grams was right. Was something more going on between Scott and Molly than they were admitting to?

Luckily, a loud burst of laughter from Ruby and Belinda distracted Grams, saving me from having to discuss Scott any further.

"What's up with those two?" Grams asked as she shoved a bite of pie into her mouth.

I rolled my eyes. "They're talking about some scavenger hunt Belinda set up for Tom. I've only heard bits and pieces of the conversation, but apparently Belinda wanted to do something extra special for Tom for their six month anniversary of dating."

Grams nearly choked on her pie. "Six month dating anniversary? I thought something like that wasn't a big deal once you were past the age of thirteen."

"I thought so, too, but you know Belinda. She's been acting like a lovesick thirteen-year-old ever since Tom moved to Sunshine

Springs."

Grams frowned, and for a few moments both of us silently munched on our pie, eavesdropping shamelessly as Belinda described in great detail the trail of clues she'd left for Tom. The clues would ultimately lead him to a golf course just outside of Sunshine Springs, where a brand new set of golf clubs would be waiting for him.

"And, of course," Belinda said cheerily, "I'll be waiting for him as well. I got myself a brand new golfing outfit. When he sees me in that cute little golfing skirt, he's going to positively swoon."

Belinda and Ruby dissolved into giggles again, and I pushed back from the café table in annoyance.

"I have to get out of here," I said to Grams. "If I have to listen to one more minute of these two talking and giggling, I'm going to lose my mind."

"You're leaving your own café in the middle of the afternoon?" Grams asked in surprise. "Surely the giggling isn't that bad." As she spoke, she snuck Sprinkles a generous piece of her pie, which I pretended not to see. I had long ago given up on trying to get her to stop feeding my dog pie, just as I'd given up on trying to get her to stop having his nails painted. I glanced down at Sprinkles' paws as he ate his pie, unsurprised to see that his nails were currently the same shade of neon green as Grams' hair.

"I have to go get more of the lemons I use for the lemon vodka pie. I buy them from a citrus farmer the next town over. He has the juiciest lemons you've ever seen, which is the secret to how flavorful my lemon pies are."

Grams brightened up at my words. "I think I know the farmer you're talking about. He also has amazing oranges. Would you mind if I came along with you? I wouldn't mind stocking up on some fresh oranges."

I grinned at her. "Sure, you can come. But won't you be sad to miss out on all the excitement here?"

Grams glanced over at Ruby and Belinda, who were caught up in their own little world. The café was a bit slow at the moment, so Ruby was taking advantage of the extra time to have an extra-long gossip session with Belinda. Grams snorted derisively.

"Pfft. There's nothing exciting going on here. In fact, there's nothing exciting going on anywhere in Sunshine Springs at the moment. Everything's as dead and dull as the grass."

I glanced out the front window at a patch of the grass Grams was speaking of. Thanks to the heat wave we'd been having, most of the grass in town had turned to a dry, dull brown color. I loved summer, but I had to admit that I was looking forward to things cooling down a bit.

"Scott said that there's no good gossip right now," I agreed. "I think he's bored out of his mind from running around town to make deliveries without any gossip to keep him going."

Grams gave Sprinkles an affectionate pat on the head, then started to stand. "Well, Scott doesn't have anything to worry about. The most exciting things always happen after the slowest weeks. I have a feeling Sunshine Springs is about to be rattled to its core."

Part of me wanted to roll my eyes at Grams for being so dramatic, but I refrained. If there was one thing Grams had proven to me over the last few months, it was that she could predict better than anyone how life would shake out in Sunshine Springs. If she said something big was coming, then odds were good that something big was coming.

Which was why, despite the heat and despite the melodic sound of Ruby's and Belinda's laughter, I shivered as I grabbed my keys and headed out the front entrance of my café.

CHAPTER TWO

Driving down a winding road through Northern California's wine country, it didn't take long for my feelings of foreboding to fade away. With brilliant sunshine and azure blue skies surrounding me, how could I be anything but happy?

And my happiness only grew after I visited my favorite citrus farmer and loaded my car up with lemons. Grams had come along with me and purchased a large basket of oranges, so our sunshine-filled drive toward home was filled with scents of fresh orange and lemon. Grams turned my car's radio to an oldies station and belted out songs at the top of her lungs, not caring that she was singing horribly off-key. And Sprinkles sat in the middle of the backseat, surrounded by oranges and lemons as he occasionally let out a joyous woof to accompany Grams' singing.

Life felt perfect in that moment, and I decided to sing along with Grams, not worrying about the fact that my voice sounded even more off-key than hers did. For a brief moment, I even closed my eyes to belt out the last note of a song.

But no sooner had I closed my eyes than Grams started screaming. My eyes flew open again as I instinctively slammed on the brakes. Fear gripped the pit of my stomach, and I half-expected that my car was going to crash into something within the next few seconds. When I'd closed my eyes, there had been nothing but a wide open, empty road in front of me. But still, I should have known better than to take my eyes off the road for even a split second. If I got into a wreck and Grams got hurt, I would never forgive myself.

All of these thoughts flew through my mind in a matter of moments, but when my car finally came to a complete stop and I got my bearings, I saw that there was still nothing but wide open road in front of me. I wasn't in any danger of crashing into anything, and I looked over at Grams in confusion. Her face had gone as white as a sheet.

"Grams? What on earth is the matter?"

My words seemed to pull her back from her shock, and she raised a hand to point over to her right. I followed the line of her pointing finger, and that's when I saw another woman running toward us—a woman who looked vaguely familiar as she waved her hands frantically and screamed out, although I had no idea what she was screaming.

"Is that...Sophia?" I asked as I put my car into park on the side of the road.

"It is indeed," Grams said as she unbuckled her seatbelt and then threw open the passenger side door of my car. I unbuckled my own seatbelt as Grams catapulted herself out of the car and started running toward Sophia. Sprinkles followed closely behind Grams, barking loudly.

I followed more slowly, stepping gingerly across the dried grass that filled the field on the side of the road. A sense of foreboding filled me as I walked toward Sophia, who was crying hysterically and trying to explain something to Grams.

Sophia Reed was one of Sunshine Springs most prominent citizens. She owned Sophia's Snips Hair Salon, which was where all of the women in Sunshine Springs went to get haircuts, beauty treatments, and gossip. I couldn't remember a time when I had seen Sophia looking unkempt or distraught. She always seemed in control of the situation, and she always kept her hair perfectly coiffed.

Not today. Today, her hair frizzed out in every possible direction. It looked as though she'd had it pulled back into a bun at one point, but now it was such a mess that it was hard to say for sure. Her makeup was running down her cheeks in messy streaks thanks to all the tears she was crying, and there were scratches visible on her arms where she'd rolled up the sleeves of her suit jacket.

The fact that she was wearing a suit jacket was strange enough on its own. I'd never seen Sophia dressed in conservative business attire. She usually favored brightly colored blouses and dresses, usually with floral prints. Even for somber occasions, like funerals, she tended to look as though she'd just returned from a tropical vacation.

Today, she looked like she'd just returned from a boring business meeting. A boring business meeting that had left her disheveled and in tears.

"Sophia!" I heard Grams exclaiming as I approached. "What on earth is the matter? What are you doing out here in a field, dressed like a banker and crying your eyes out?"

Sophia cried even harder, and Sprinkles ran in circles around her. His frantic, excited barking only added to the chaos of the moment.

"He's...not moving!" Sophia managed to say. "He's not moving at all. I think he needs a doctor."

Grams and I exchanged a worried glance. I was already reaching for my cell phone as Grams turned back to Sophia. If someone out here was so sick or wounded that they couldn't even move, then I was going to need to call an ambulance.

"Who's not moving, dear?" Grams asked. I marveled at how calm and soothing she managed to make her voice sound.

"Tom! He's lying over there by that grove of lemon trees with a big gash in the back of his head. It's bleeding quite a bit. I...I think he needs a doctor."

Sophia wrung her hands hysterically, and I took off running in the direction of the lemon trees she'd pointed toward. I was already dialing 911 to call an ambulance, but when I saw the unmoving body, I had a feeling that no ambulance was going to be able to help the heap of a man lying crumpled beneath the lemon tree.

I winced and felt my stomach turn as I went to check the man's pulse. As I suspected, there was no pulse to be found. As much as I didn't want to look, I forced myself to glance at what was visible of the man's face.

Sophia had been right. It was Tom. Tom Schmidt, who was supposed to be following the clues of a scavenger hunt that would lead him to the nearby golf course and a new set of golf clubs. It looked like he wasn't going to be playing any games with those new golf clubs, and it also looked like he was never going to have the chance to see Belinda in her new golfing outfit.

Tom Schmidt looked very, very dead.

"911, what is your emergency?"

The voice squawking in my ear through my cell phone startled me so badly that I nearly dropped my phone. Once I regained my composure, I let out a long, weary sigh.

"Yes, this is Izzy James. I need to report a death."

There was a pause on the other end of the line, and I could only imagine what the operator must be thinking. Everyone in Sunshine Springs knew that I'd been involved in several murder investigations since my arrival in town earlier in the year. At one point, I myself had even been a suspect in one of the murder investigations. I'd been acquitted, and had even helped solve that crime, but I'm sure folks must have thought it was strange how often I managed to get tangled up in these sorts of messes. I winced as I thought about what Mitch McCoy, the local sheriff, was going to think when he heard that I was wrapped up in this case as well.

Of course, this might not be a murder. It was possible there had been some sort of accident here. Perhaps Tom had fallen and hit his head, or some other benign explanation. I told myself not to get too worked up about things yet, but my mind was already spinning. The gash on the back of Tom's head would had to have come from a pretty bad fall, if it was indeed due to a fall. I glanced up at the lemon trees near Tom, and saw that one of them had several broken branches. Had Tom been climbing that tree and fallen down? That would explain the broken branches and the gash on his head. But it didn't exactly explain why Tom was climbing the tree in the first place, or why Sophia was out here.

I looked nervously over at Sophia. I wouldn't have called her my favorite person in Sunshine Springs, but I liked her well enough. She was a horrible gossip, but she did seem to care about her fellow citizens. I knew she would squeeze people in for appointments at the salon, even when she had to stay late or open early to do so. And the senior discounts she offered to Sunshine Springs' elderly residents meant that anyone Grams' age practically got haircuts for free. Surely, she wasn't the type to hurt someone.

Then again, if the last few months had taught me anything, it was that people weren't always who they seemed to be. After I finished speaking with the 911 operator, I gulped and narrowed my eyes at Sophia. She and Grams were slowly walking toward the spot where Tom lay lifeless on the ground.

"What happened out here?" I couldn't quite keep the accusing tone out of my voice, but Sophia was so distraught that she didn't seem to notice my tone. She looked at me with wide, tearful eyes, and shook her head in a gesture of disbelief.

"I...I don't know. I saw Tom and needed to talk to him, so I stopped up the road and got out of my car to chase him down. But he was rushing across the field so quickly that I had a hard time catching up with him. I thought I'd lost him and was about to give up and head back to my car when I noticed what looked like a person crumpled up beneath the tree here. I came to look and found him here like this."

Sophia dissolved into sobs again, and Grams gave me a look that said I shouldn't be interrogating her.

I bit my lower lip in frustration as Grams gently guided Sophia away from Tom's lifeless body and toward a large rock that made a good makeshift seat. Once Sophia was seated, Grams patted her lightly on the back, whispering to her in soothing tones that everything was going to be alright.

I knew that Grams was right, and that it wasn't my place to question Sophia. But, as usual, my burning curiosity was getting the best of me. I wanted to know more about what had happened here, and it was all I could do to keep silent until the police and the ambulance arrived.

As expected, when the paramedics arrived they declared Tom dead on arrival. I tried not to watch as they checked his vitals, but I couldn't quite force myself to look away. When they looked up at Sheriff Mitch and shook their heads sadly, I knew it was official. Tom was gone.

I tried not to think about how Belinda was going to take the news. I hadn't been the biggest fan of Tom. He'd always seemed arrogant and aloof to me, which wasn't the best fit for a friendly small town like Sunshine Springs. But it still came as a shock to see that he was dead, and I felt badly for Belinda. She was obviously over the moon about him, and this was going to be a hard blow for her to take.

I went to sit by Grams and Sophia as the police taped off the area and started taking pictures. I knew they had to cover every possibility, but I couldn't imagine that this was a murder. Tom was new in town, and he had received a cool reception due to the fact that he was seen as a wife stealer. But surely, no one had disliked him enough to actually kill him. Even Frank, Belinda's ex-husband who had every reason to hate Tom, couldn't possibly have done this. At least, I didn't think he could have. Frank wasn't the vengeful type, and as far as I could tell, he had done his best to move on and make the best of a difficult situation.

But when Mitch finally finished talking to his detectives and made his way over to where Grams, Sophia, and I were sitting, one look at the sheriff's face told me everything I needed to know. This death had not been an accident.

Mitch cracked his knuckles loudly, as he often did when he was thinking deeply. Many times, the sound annoyed me. But just then, I found it comforting. The world felt like chaos at the moment, and the sound of Mitch's knuckles cracking brought a welcome familiarity. I smiled weakly up at him, trying to think of what might be appropriate to say in a situation such as the one I found myself in. But before I could speak, Mitch was shaking his head at me and speaking.

"I swear, Izzy. You somehow find a way to mix yourself up in my crime scenes every time."

"Is that what this is?" I asked. "A crime scene?"

I didn't want to believe that Tom had truly been murdered, but Mitch was nodding his head. "This is definitely a crime scene. The coroner will have to confirm things with an autopsy, of course. But it doesn't take much of an expert to see that the gash on the back of Tom's head didn't come from a fall. It came from someone stabbing him with something."

"Is that so?" I felt a little woozy, and I put my hand on the cool rock beneath me to try to steady myself. "I tried not to look that closely at the gash, to be honest."

Mitch let out a long sigh. "Well, I'm glad you spared yourself that much, at least. But knowing you, I'm sure you'll be sticking your nose deep into this case before long. I'd tell you to stay out of things, but I know by now that it would be a waste of breath."

I shrugged my shoulders and gave him a sheepish grin. "I can't help it if trouble constantly finds me."

Mitch only grunted in response, but then pointed to Sophia. "And what about her? How did she end up tangled up in all this trouble?"

I glanced at Sophia, who was staring listlessly off into space at the moment. She'd finally stopped crying, but she still looked horribly upset. I couldn't blame her. It wasn't every day that you ran across a dead body, and I imagined that the whole experience must have been quite upsetting for her. I myself wasn't too thrilled about the unexpected twist in my day, although I was doing my best to put on a brave face.

"I don't really know how she was involved in all of this," I said, lowering my voice in hopes that Sophia wouldn't notice I was talking about her. "I was driving home from picking up lemons for my lemon pie, and all of a sudden Grams screamed. I looked over and saw Sophia on the side of the road, looking like she'd just seen a ghost. She hasn't said much about what actually happened."

Mitch frowned and glanced over at Sophia as well. "I'll have to get a statement from her, but I'm not sure how coherent she is right now. She looks like a mess, which is unusual for Sophia."

I grunted my agreement, and Grams put a protective arm around Sophia. Grams didn't like it when Mitch tried to get statements from people while they were still distraught, but I understood that Mitch had to do his job. Sophia had just been the first person to arrive at a murder scene, and Mitch needed to know what she had seen.

"Come on, Grams," I said, pulling on her arm. "Let's take a quick walk to stretch our legs while Mitch talks to Sophia. He'll be as quick as possible."

Grams looked like she might protest, but after a moment's consideration she nodded. "Fine. But Mitch, you be nice to Sophia." She wagged a warning finger in Mitch's direction, and I dragged her away before Mitch could make some indignant reply. Grams could be feisty, and many in Sunshine Springs were afraid of her. But Mitch had never been intimidated by Grams, and the last thing I wanted to deal with right now was watching their two stubborn heads collide.

"He better not be accusing Sophia of murder!" Grams fumed as I continued to drag her away, hoping Mitch hadn't heard her remarks. He hated being told how to run his investigations, and he looked like he was in the mood to fight right now.

Besides, I had to admit that my own stomach was clenching up in anxious, confused knots over the fact that Sophia was here. I couldn't bring myself to believe that she herself had murdered Tom. She might be the town's biggest gossip, but she was still a decent human being. I couldn't believe that she would actually kill someone.

But then, who had killed Tom? Had Sophia seen the true murderer?

I only half-listened to Grams as she ranted on about Mitch. My brain was far too occupied with questions about the murder itself to worry about how Mitch was conducting his investigation, and I felt a small rush of excitement a few minutes later when Mitch waved me back over. Had he learned who had killed Tom? And was he going to share that information with me?

I should have known better than to hope for so much. It turned out that Mitch merely wanted to know if I would be willing to drive Sophia home.

"I think I've gotten as much information from her as I'm going to get right now," Mitch said. "She's too worked up to give me coherent answers to my questions."

"Sure, I can take her home," I said, then couldn't resist adding, "Did she see what happened here?"

Mitch gave me a sharp warning look. "Izzy, please. Don't start trying to solve this crime. Whoever did this is dangerous, and I don't want you to get hurt. That gash on the back of Tom's head wasn't pretty, and I don't want you to end up with a gash like that on your own head."

I tried to laugh off his comment. "Oh, please. No one has any reason to want to bash my head in."

Mitch did not laugh. "Well I don't know what reason they had to bash in Tom's head, but there he is. All bashed in."

I shivered, and stopped laughing. "Right. Good point. I'll go ahead and get Sophia home."

"I appreciate it," Mitch said. "I have enough other things to worry about right now besides taking a hysterical woman home. I have a feeling I'll be dealing with another hysterical woman soon enough."

I raised a questioning eyebrow. "Who?"

"Belinda Simmons," Mitch said in a tone of voice that said this should have been obvious. "I'll need to get a statement from her as well, to make sure she wasn't involved in killing Tom somehow. I can't see her doing something like this, either, but I need to cover all my bases. I already sent one of my officers to her house to deliver the news."

But Mitch was suddenly interrupted by the roar of an engine and screeching of tires. Everyone at the crime scene looked up and saw a white sports coupe coming to a stop in a cloud of dust on the side of the road. Moments later, Belinda Simmons herself jumped out of the car and started running toward the crime scene as she let out a series of frenzied shrieks.

I glanced over at Mitch, whose eyes had widened as he looked at Belinda.

"You might want to tell your officer not to bother going by her house," I said. "Looks like she's already heard the news."

"Looks like it," Mitch said with a sigh. "And it looks like you need to get Sophia out of here right now."

"But—" I started to protest. I didn't want to leave in the middle of Belinda's arrival. I might learn something interesting about the case.

Mitch didn't even let me finish my sentence. He held up a hand to silence me, and shook his head. "Izzy, give it a rest, okay? I don't need your help playing detective right now. I need your help getting Sophia home."

I was about to protest again, but when I glanced over at Sophia, I thought better of it. She looked like she was on the verge of a complete breakdown, and I figured it was better to get her home. As much as I wanted to stay and hear what Belinda might know about what had happened to Tom, I knew Mitch was right. Sophia needed to get home.

"Come on," I said to Grams and Sprinkles as I gently reached to grab Sophia's arm. "Let's get out of here."

But even as I led a sobbing Sophia to my car, I couldn't resist constantly glancing back to see what Belinda was doing. At the moment, she was standing right in front of Mitch, gesturing wildly. She was yelling so loudly that I could easily make out what she was saying, even though there was now a good amount of distance between us.

"He wasn't even supposed to be out here! Those clues are wrong! Someone changed them!"

I felt a chill run down my spine. Had Belinda's scavenger hunt been intended to bring harm to Tom? She was wearing her ridiculous new golf outfit with the frilly skirt, but perhaps she had known all along that he would never see her in it. After all, she had written out the clues. She knew exactly where he would be, and when. Had she sent him to this deserted grove of lemon trees to kill him off when she thought no one was looking?

But then how had Sophia ended up here? Was she involved somehow? I looked back at Sophia, and then at Belinda again. When

I looked at Belinda, however, Mitch caught my eye and glared at me. He was annoyed with me for still being there, and I turned to hurry away.

But even though I was leaving, I knew one thing for sure: I would be digging deeper into this murder case. My curiosity had been piqued, and I was already planning how I could find out more about what had happened.

If Mitch didn't like it, that was his problem.

CHAPTER THREE

There was no ignoring the truth right in front of my eyes: Sophia Reed's house looked like a disaster zone. I had never been to her house before, but given how orderly and pristine she kept her hair salon, I had expected her home to be neat and clean as well.

Far from it.

Dirty dishes had been piled high on every available surface in the kitchen. The dining room table was covered with piles of paper, most of which looked like unopened mail. The blinds on the back window were torn, and I had to constantly resist the urge to sneeze—dust clung to every available surface.

The Sophia I knew from the hair salon would have been horribly embarrassed to have a guest see her house in such a state, but the Sophia in front of me hardly seemed to notice. She sank into an armchair in the living room, sending up a cloud of dust as she did. Then she turned to me and shook her head in a gesture of disbelief.

"I can't believe Tom's dead. This is not at all how I thought my day was going to go."

"Mine either," I quipped. I suddenly wished that I had brought Grams along with me to Sophia's house. Grams' house was on the way to Sophia's so I had dropped her off before bringing Sophia home. I'd even let Grams keep Sprinkles for the night, because I knew she felt shaken up by the murder, even if she wouldn't admit it. Having Sprinkles nearby would help Grams' feel more secure.

But even though I was happy that Grams was safe and resting at home, I wished she could have seen the mess in Sophia's house with her own eyes. I had a feeling that no one would believe me if I told them that Sophia was living like this, but the mess made me uneasy.

It didn't fit Sophia's personality, at least not the Sophia I thought I knew. What else was Sophia hiding from everyone? Surely, she wasn't hiding the fact that she was capable of murder.

Was she?

I decided that I didn't want to leave until I'd had the chance to ask her some questions. Mitch may not have gotten very much out of her, but Mitch didn't know how to talk to a woman. I had a few ideas on how to get Sophia to talk.

"Can I make you something to eat? Or perhaps some tea?" I didn't wait for permission before I marched into the kitchen to start looking for some food that I could quickly prepare for Sophia. If I could convince her to eat, she might relax enough to speak with me for a bit.

And even if she wouldn't talk to me, she still needed to eat. She looked entirely too skinny, if you asked me. I'd noticed a while ago that she was losing weight, and at first I'd been happy for her, thinking she must have found a diet that would work well for her. But now, she had taken the weight loss a bit too far. She was getting down to skin and bones.

"Just a tea, dear," Sophia's weary voice called to me from the living room. "I don't think I have much in the house to eat at the moment."

As I opened cupboard after cupboard, I saw that she wasn't kidding. Her cupboards were bare, and as dusty as the rest of her house. In fact, I couldn't even find any tea. There was a bag of stale coffee grounds, a bag of flour that I was afraid to even look at for fear it might be full of worms, and there were a few cans of beans.

With a frown on my face, I left the kitchen and went to talk to Sophia.

"Have you been eating anything at all lately?" I asked. "You have no food here, and it looks like you haven't had food here for quite some time."

Sophia looked up at me dully, as though I was speaking a foreign language that she couldn't quite comprehend. I was beginning to think that leaving her here alone might not be the best idea, as she looked like she had gone into a state of shock.

"Sophia?" I tried again. "Should I order you some takeout,

perhaps? There's no food here at all. Not even tea."

"Oh dear," Sophia said. "I'm out of tea now, too? I thought I still had a bit left. Oh well. It's alright, Izzy. I'm not that hungry, anyway, so there's no need to order me food. I've just been too busy to get to the grocery store, but I guess I'll have to make time for it this week. It should be easier now that..."

She trailed off, and I waited impatiently for a moment before prompting her. "Now that what?"

But she merely waved a dismissive hand in my direction. "Never mind. I'll just have some water for tonight, and go to the store tomorrow."

I frowned in her direction. I had decided to hang around for my own selfish purposes, because I wanted to know what she might know about Tom's murder. But now, I was truly worried about her. It had been more than just a week or two since she'd been grocery shopping. She'd eaten through almost everything in her pantry. And grocery shopping didn't take that much time. Yes, the hair salon was busy, but it wasn't as though she was working at some stock broker firm in New York City. Surely, she had some time. She couldn't have been too busy to make a quick run for food at some point within the last few weeks.

Was it possible that she couldn't afford food? But that didn't make much sense, either. Sophia's hair salon was one of the most successful businesses in Sunshine Springs. She might not be as rich as Theo, who owned the Sunshine Springs Winery, but she must have been pretty well-off, nonetheless. Something strange was going on here, but it wasn't my place to pry. The part of me that had been raised to be polite told me that I should leave and let Sophia save face.

I chewed my lower lip for a moment, but then shook my head. Was there anything truly polite about letting Sophia go hungry?

"I think we should order some food," I said gently. "I'm hungry, too. What if I order us a pizza to share?"

I half-expected Sophia to protest, but instead she looked relieved. "Oh, okay. But only if you're hungry, too."

"I'm starving," I said with a smile. It wasn't exactly true. Although I hadn't eaten for a few hours, witnessing the aftermath of a murder had left me without much of an appetite. But if pretending to be hungry meant that I could convince Sophia to eat, then I would pretend to be hungry.

A little less than an hour later, Sophia was hungrily chowing down on a large slice of pepperoni pizza and taking long sips from a glass of soda. I'd ordered the party package which included appetizers and a two liter bottle of soda, and Sophia was taking advantage of the wealth of food. She was acting like she hadn't eaten in a month. Maybe she hadn't.

I told myself I was going to mind my own business for once, and that I wouldn't pry Sophia for information about the real reason she hadn't been grocery shopping. I even told myself it was better if I didn't press her for information on Tom's murder. But it turned out that I didn't have to ask any questions. After Sophia ate a couple of breadsticks and a slice of pizza, she was in quite a talkative mood.

"I just can't believe what happened to Tom! I never really liked the guy, but I can't believe that someone would murder him!"

"Maybe he wasn't murdered," I said, even though Mitch had been quite convinced that the death had been a homicide. "His body looked quite crumpled, which meant that he had probably fallen from one of those lemon trees. Maybe it was the fall that killed him."

Sophia shook her head. "I don't think so. I saw that gash on his head. I don't know what he could possibly have fallen on that would have left a gash that horrible."

"I see your point, but I think falling from a tree could do quite a bit of damage, even if all you hit was the ground."

Sophia shrugged, but still looked unconvinced. If I was honest, I didn't believe Tom's death had been an accident, either. Tom had been relatively young, and he was strong and healthy. Climbing a tree shouldn't have been all that difficult for him, and lemon trees weren't that big. If he had somehow managed to fall, odds were good he would have only been injured, not killed.

"What was he doing in that lemon tree, anyway?" Sophia asked.

"Looking for the next clue in Belinda's scavenger hunt," I said as I picked up a breadstick and munched it absentmindedly for a few moments.

"Scavenger hunt?" Sophia sounded completely lost, but a cynical part of me wondered if she was putting on a show. It still seemed odd to me that she had just happened to be out near a deserted grove of lemon trees in the middle of the day. Had she known about the clues of the scavenger hunt, and had she known Tom would be there?

I watched her face carefully as I started to explain. "Belinda wanted to do something extra-romantic for Tom for their six-month dating anniversary, so she set up a scavenger hunt for him. She wanted him to follow clues that would eventually take him to a golf course where she would be waiting to gift him a new set of golf clubs."

Sophia stared at me in disbelief, looking truly coherent for the first time since I'd seen her on the side of the road by the lemon grove. "Are you kidding me? Belinda wanted to do something special for a six month *dating* anniversary?"

I shrugged. "I thought it was a bit over the top, too. But you know how infatuated Belinda was with Tom. She practically worshipped the ground he walked on."

Sophia made a sound that was somewhere between a snort and a laugh. "Maybe if she had worked that hard on her relationship with Frank, her marriage wouldn't have fallen apart."

My jaw dropped in disbelief before I could stop myself. Sophia was known for always having the latest gossip, but she usually shared it in a way that managed to be reasonably kind. I had never before heard her speak so disdainfully about another Sunshine Springs resident, and I couldn't hide my shock.

"What?" Sophia asked in a defensive tone. "It's true. She gave Frank a hard time about everything when all he ever did was work hard to provide for her. Then this Tom jerk comes along and Belinda can't get enough of him. I have no idea what she saw in him."

I blinked a few times, unsure of what to say. Sophia wasn't acting like herself. Between the chaotic state of her house, the lack of food in her pantry, and the disdainful comments about Belinda, I felt like I was seeing a completely different Sophia Reed than the warm, bubbly woman who ran Sophia's Snips Hair Salon and Spa.

An uneasy feeling grew in the pit of my stomach as I mulled over everything Sophia had just said. Had she been angry enough at Belinda to harm Tom? I found it hard to believe she would do something like that, and she had seemed genuinely surprised when I told her about the scavenger hunt. But what if it was all an act, and Sophia Reed had gone crazy and turned into a murderer? She still hadn't said anything that would explain why she had been out on a deserted stretch of road in the middle of the day—a deserted stretch of road where a man had been murdered.

I shivered involuntarily, then told myself to calm down. Sophia was practically a pillar in the Sunshine Springs community. Even if she was going through a tough time personally for some reason, she would never kill someone. There had to be another reason for her strange behavior.

But even though I couldn't believe Sophia was a murderer, I couldn't shake the feeling that she knew more about Tom and his death than she was admitting. I wanted to beg her to tell me what she knew, but I could tell she was nearing the point of total exhaustion. To be honest, so was I.

I decided I would head home to rest for the evening, but first thing in the morning I would call up Sophia's Snips and book an appointment for a haircut with Sophia.

There were clues to be tracked down, and I was going to find them.

CHAPTER FOUR

Even though I felt exhausted down to my bones, I lay in bed wide awake for hours. My mind wouldn't stop spinning, trying to put together the puzzle pieces on how and why Tom had been murdered. But the more I thought about it, the more confused I became. There just weren't enough pieces to make anything close to a complete puzzle, and I knew I had a lot of work ahead of me if I wanted to solve this murder case.

At two a.m., I found myself staring down at my phone, annoyed with the realization that Molly hadn't texted me. I'd sent her a message as soon as I got home from Sophia's house, explaining everything I knew about the case thus far. Molly always helped me out when I was chasing down murder suspects, and I didn't want to take the chance that she would hear about Tom's murder from anyone other than me. I could hardly wait to discuss with her the meager clues I had so far.

But Molly didn't reply. At first, I assumed that she must have still been in the movie theater. But by the time two a.m. rolled around, I knew she just wasn't answering. That probably meant that she and Scott had decided to go for drinks after the movie, and Molly had been too distracted to see that she had a text from me. I tried not to be too jealous at the thought of them hanging out and having fun without me, but the events of the day had put me in a rotten mood. It was hard not to feel rottener over my best friend being too busy to text me back.

"I am being downright ridiculous," I said aloud to myself as I sat up in bed. That was the moment that I decided I needed to get up and do something useful. Tossing and turning in bed wasn't putting me in a better mood. Quite the opposite, in fact. It was only making me dwell on everything that had gone wrong the day before.

I made the split second decision to get up and head to the café to bake some pies. I still hadn't unloaded the boxes of lemons from my car, so I figured I might as well take them down to the café and see if I could actually bake enough lemon vodka pies to keep up with demand for once. While I was at the café, I could make myself a good, strong espresso. I had the feeling that I wasn't going to be sleeping any tonight, so the caffeine would be a welcome boost.

The entire world was quiet as I parked my car on Main Street and unlocked the front door of my café. Even the late night wine bars had closed up by then, and I felt like I was the only one stirring in town. I loved the feeling of being the only one awake—of being alone with the flour and sugar that I would craft into dozens of perfect pies. I only wished that I had kept Sprinkles with me tonight instead of leaving him with Grams. He made the perfect companion for a late night or early morning baking session. I loved the sound of his tail lazily thumping against the cool tile floor as I worked.

But even without Sprinkles here in the café, I felt like I was in my happy place. I breathed in deeply, savoring the lingering sweetness that always seemed to hang in the air here.

And then, I got to work. I propped the front door open and carried the boxes of lemons inside. I would put whatever lemons I didn't need for tonight's baking into the industrial refrigerator for the pies I would make later in the week. I should have stored the lemons this way as soon as I got back to Sunshine Springs, but I'd been too distracted by everything that had gone on with Sophia to stop by the café earlier in the night.

Once the lemons were stored properly, I went to make myself an espresso. Normally, I would have needed to wait about twenty minutes for the machine to properly warm up before I could make myself a latte, but Ruby had forgotten to turn the machine off when she closed up for the night. I felt a slight twinge of annoyance when I realized this, but I couldn't be too mad at her. After all, her error had ended up working in my favor, since I wouldn't need to wait for my espresso.

Once my latte was ready, I decided to check on the day's sales to see how much money the café had made after I left. There had been a small lull in customers when I'd left to go buy the lemons, but usually the café had another rush later in the afternoon.

When I looked at the sales for the day, however, I realized that there had never been another rush after I left. In fact, there were hardly any sales for the rest of the afternoon. I frowned, and looked at the list of leftover pie. There were quite a few that hadn't been sold. My frown deepened as I went to the refrigerator and saw what I had been too distracted to notice when I was carrying the lemons in: a stack of pie boxes, filled with unsold pies.

I chewed my lower lip as I left the refrigerator. Had the day really been that slow after I left, or had Ruby somehow driven away customers? I felt a bit disloyal to my new employee for even asking myself that question, but it had to be asked. Ruby was usually such a good employee that it was hard to imagine her causing trouble for customers. But then, it was also hard to imagine an afternoon with almost zero sales. The heat wave meant that it still felt like summer around Sunshine Springs, and there were still quite a lot of tourists. That meant that I was selling quite a bit of pie still.

I mulled over the sales numbers for a few more moments, then shrugged and decided to let the matter go. The overall sales for the day had been good, and the slow afternoon might have been a mere fluke. Even if Ruby had gotten overwhelmed for some reason and had driven away customers, it was just one afternoon. My pie shop could handle one afternoon of slow sales.

What I couldn't handle was losing my only employee. I would give Ruby the benefit of the doubt, because what choice did I really have? I had spent countless hours looking for someone to help me out at the pie shop. The very thought of starting over with a search for another employee made my head hurt.

Feeling a bit less enthusiastic than I had when I first arrived at the café, I quickly drained the rest of my latte and decided to get to work. Tomorrow would be a better day. If nothing else, at least I wouldn't have to deal with seeing a murdered man lying beneath a lemon tree.

At least, I hoped I wouldn't. One never knew what the day was going to bring here in Sunshine Springs.

I turned my attention to prepping ingredients for my pies. I would make several batches of lemon vodka pies, but I'd also make some nonalcoholic lemon chiffon pies. Not everyone who came in wanted boozy pie, and I liked to have options to keep everyone happy.

I soon lost myself in my work, measuring and mixing ingredients, and humming happily to myself. The espresso hit my system and gave me a jolt of energy, and I felt I was getting into a good baking rhythm. Life was good. I probably wouldn't get a wink of sleep tonight, which meant I'd be exhausted during the café's opening hours tomorrow, but at least there would be plenty of pie.

I was working at a nice pace, still humming happily, when a loud crash sounded from the front of my café. I froze with my hands in a bowlful of dough, trying to remember whether I'd left anything out front that could possibly have fallen over.

I couldn't think of anything. I knew with certainty that I'd carried all the boxes of lemons back to the refrigerator. The only thing out front was tables and chairs, and none of them were likely to fall over spontaneously.

My heart stuck in my throat. Someone was in my café.

I was sure of it. That crash had to have been a chair falling over, and it had fallen over because someone ran into it. I desperately wished that I had Sprinkles with me, but wishing wasn't going to change the fact that he was at Grams' house and I was here alone.

Had I forgotten to lock the front door? I found that hard to believe. I was so methodical about dead-bolting the front entrance when I came in to bake each morning. But it didn't really matter whether I'd left the door unlocked, or whether someone had picked the lock. The bottom line was that I was alone in my café with an intruder.

I stood perfectly still for several long moments, my hands clenched into fists around the pie crust dough in front of me as I listened for any other sounds. I was hoping that somehow I had imagined the crash, and that if I went out to the front of the café and flipped all the lights on that I would find the place empty.

But then, I heard the sound of footsteps. The sound was soft, as though someone was tiptoeing. But in the perfect stillness of the otherwise empty café, there was no mistaking that the sound was indeed footsteps. I felt my heart pounding in my chest as I tried to imagine why anyone would break into a café in the wee hours of the morning. Hopefully, the intruder just wanted money, but I hadn't forgotten that there was a murderer on the loose in Sunshine Springs.

Was that murderer coming after me for some reason?

I gulped, and turned to run to my office. I would slam the door behind me and lock it, then dial 911. Hopefully, the locked door would keep the intruder at bay until the cops had time to arrive.

I felt tears forming in my eyes as I fumbled with the lock to the office. With my shaky hands, it took me three attempts to get it locked, but I finally managed. My sticky, dough-covered hands left flour residue all over the handle, but I'd worry about that later. Right now, I needed to survive.

I grabbed the cordless handset for the phone in my office, and started trying to dial. My sticky fingers had just managed to hit the number nine when the intruder spoke.

"Izzy? Is that you? Are you okay?"

The familiar, concerned-sounding voice filled me with a rush of relief and exasperation all at the same time.

"Ruby?"

"Yeah, it's Ruby," came the voice from the other side of the door. "What are you doing holed up in your office while pies are baking in the oven? Are you alright?"

I set down the phone, not sure whether to laugh or cry—or both—and then I fumbled to unlock the door. Despite my current feelings of exasperation toward Ruby, I had to admit that I was relieved to see it was her standing there instead of some coldblooded murderer. I almost could have hugged her in that moment, especially since she had such a genuine expression of concern on her face.

"What in the world are you doing here at this time of the morning?" I asked, wiping my hands on my apron and trying to regain some small semblance of dignity. I must have looked like a complete nut case, with my hair frizzing out from its ponytail, my apron covered in dough, and my eyes still a bit wet from the tears of panic that had been forming just moments ago.

"I couldn't sleep," Ruby said. "So I thought I'd surprise you by coming out to the café and getting a head start on the day's baking. But it looks like you beat me to it. I didn't expect you here quite this early."

I took a deep breath as I felt my heart slowly returning to normal. "I'm earlier than usual, but I couldn't sleep either. Let me guess: you heard about Tom's murder?"

Ruby nodded her head solemnly. "Belinda is beside herself, the poor thing. She had to spend quite a bit of time down at the police station giving a statement. She was texting me the whole time, and as soon as I closed up the café I went to be with her. I'm not sure how much comfort I was really able to offer her, but I tried."

I felt my cheeks turning red with shame as I realized that the afternoon's low sales, and Ruby's absentmindedness in forgetting to turn off the espresso machine, were probably all due to the fact that Ruby had been distracted by Belinda. Could I blame her for wanting to focus on her friend? If I'd had a friend stuck down at the police station giving a statement because that friend's boyfriend had just been murdered, I'd probably be a bit distracted, too.

"It's been a rough day for Belinda," I said sympathetically. "But it must have been rough for you as well. How are you holding up?"

For the first time since I'd known her, I saw a flash of vulnerability in Ruby's eyes. Ruby always acted bubbly and strong, but right now, I could see that the toll of taking care of Belinda was weighing her down.

"I've been better," Ruby admitted. "But I guess I can't complain too much. I'm alive and safe, and that's more than can be said for poor Tom."

Tears started to form in Ruby's eyes, and I reached over to squeeze her arm. "This has been a bit of a shocking day, hasn't it? No wonder you can't sleep. Tell you what: I'll make us both lattes, and then we can tackle this baking together. Whenever something is upsetting me, there's nothing quite as therapeutic as baking a bunch of pies."

Ruby smiled gratefully and nodded. "That sounds perfect."

Fifteen minutes later, Ruby and I were both feeling refreshed after indulging in strong lattes. Ruby put on an apron, and soon we were both elbow deep in pie dough.

For a while, we worked in silence. I knew that Ruby must have some inside information on Tom's murder, since she'd spent time down at the police station with Belinda. But I forced myself to keep quiet and not pester Ruby with questions. The poor girl had been through enough today, and as much as I wanted to know what she knew, I didn't want to force her to talk about things if she wasn't ready.

Luckily for me, after a short time of prepping pies in silence, Ruby seemed ready to talk. She looked up at me with sad eyes and shook her head forlornly.

"I feel so badly for Belinda. She was so excited about that scavenger hunt, and then it ended in Tom's death. She feels like it was her fault that he was murdered, even though I told her about a thousand times that she can't blame herself for it. How was she supposed to know that someone would be waiting for him along the path of clues to take him out?"

"She couldn't know," I said. "But it sounds like someone did more than just lie in wait on the path of clues Belinda had set out."

Ruby frowned. "What do you mean by that?"

"I mean that it sounds like someone actually changed some of the clues. They knew Tom was going on a scavenger hunt, and they somehow got a hold of the clues Belinda had made for him and changed one of them to direct him to the lemon grove. I was still at the murder scene when Belinda arrived, and she was crying hysterically and saying that someone had changed the clues around. But surely, she must have explained all of that to you while you were down at the police station."

Ruby's eyes widened, and she shook her head. "No, she never mentioned anything about that. All she told me was that someone had somehow figured out that Tom was doing a scavenger hunt and had killed him along the way. She didn't tell me that the clues had changed."

Now I was the one frowning. It seemed odd that Belinda hadn't mentioned the changing clues to Ruby. After all, Ruby had become one of Belinda's best friends, and it sounded like Ruby had spent quite a bit of time down at the police station with Belinda. Why wouldn't Belinda have shared such a major detail with Ruby?

I felt a chill going down my spine. If Belinda was hiding such an important detail from Ruby, then what else was she hiding, and from whom? A few weeks ago, Belinda had been a suspect in the murder of Edgar Bates, who had been Sunshine Springs' oldest citizen up until his death. She'd been cleared of that murder, but I couldn't resist thinking that there was something sinister about the fact that she was once again closely connected to a murder. Was it possible that she wasn't so innocent this time?

"Are you alright?" Ruby asked.

I looked up to see her staring at me with an expression of concern, and I did my best to paste a wide smile onto my face. "I'm fine. Just overwhelmed by everything that's happened today."

I didn't want to trouble Ruby with my worries over Belinda's innocence. After all, I didn't have much to base those worries on. Maybe I had misheard Belinda back at the crime scene. Or perhaps Belinda herself had been mistaken, and had later realized that the clues hadn't been changed after all. It was even possible that Belinda had just been so overwhelmed that she hadn't had the mental energy to explain the changed clues to Ruby. There were several possibilities for why Ruby didn't know about the changed clues, and odds were good that the reason had nothing to do with Belinda being the murderer.

"Maybe we shouldn't talk about the murder anymore," Ruby said gently. "I don't want to upset you further, and, to be honest, talking about it is only making me more upset, too."

I almost argued with Ruby, thinking that I should come up with some explanation for why it was better to talk about it and get it all out of our system. But when I looked at Ruby's pale face, I felt guilty. She'd had a harder day than I had, in many ways. This was probably the first time she'd been so close to a murder, and she must have been exhausted from spending so much time at the station trying to cheer up Belinda. It wasn't fair for me to continue to push the subject on her.

Yes, I wanted to learn as much as I could about Tom's death, but I could find out what I wanted to know another way. Scott always knew the latest town gossip, and I had his number on speed dial. Besides, I already had an appointment scheduled at Sophia's Snips for later that day. Spending time at the hair salon guaranteed that I would be kept up to date on the latest news and gossip. There was no need for me to traumatize Ruby any further.

"You're right," I said, giving Ruby a more genuine smile this time. "There's no need to keep rehashing everything. Let's focus on getting these pies baked."

And that's exactly what we did. For the next few hours, we baked dozens of lemon vodka pies. When we finished, there was still an hour before the café opened, and Ruby encouraged me to take a quick cat nap in my office. She ended up letting me sleep for a full two hours, only waking me when the morning rush became too much to handle by herself. I was still tired, but even two hours of sleep did wonders to make me feel more alive. I quickly donned my apron and went to help Ruby. She had turned out to be an amazing employee, and I happily overlooked the fact that she'd accidentally left the espresso machine on the day before. Whatever small mistakes she'd made were quickly erased in my mind when I saw how hard she was working to keep the morning rush at bay.

I stepped behind the espresso machine to take over all the morning latte orders, and I smiled as I looked out over the line that snaked all the way out the front door. It still amazed me how successful my little pie café had become, and how quickly my dreams had come true.

I was about to turn back toward the espresso machine when I caught sight of Molly squeezing her way through the front door. She was tightly gripping her red leather purse in one hand, and her cell phone in the other. I realized in that moment that I still hadn't received a reply from her to any of my texts. I might have acted miffed at her about that, if not for the fact that the expression on her face worried me.

Molly, who always had a smile for everyone, did not look happy. In fact, she looked quite distressed.

CHAPTER FIVE

As usual, Molly bypassed the line and came straight to where I stood behind the front counter. She peered over the espresso machine at me and looked nervously around, as though afraid she was being followed.

"Are you alright?" I asked. I had to admit that I was a bit angry that she still hadn't answered any of my texts from the night before. But that anger took a backseat to my concern over my best friend. I wasn't sure what was making her look so distressed, but if there was something I could do to help, then I would. That's what friends were for, right?

Molly let out a long, dramatic sigh. "I'm fine, but I need to talk to you. Do you have a minute?"

I gave Molly an incredulous look. "Are you serious? You know how busy the café gets in the morning, and you can see the line out the door. Does it look like I have a minute?"

My voice was sharper than I intended, and Molly winced. That made me wince a bit. I wasn't trying to be too harsh on my friend, but it *had* been a bit of a ridiculous question.

"Right," Molly said sheepishly. "I know you're busy. But I guess I thought I might be able to squeeze in a few minutes of conversation. I should have known better. I'm sorry I bothered you."

I was tempted to make a smart retort about how if she'd wanted to talk to me that badly, then she should have replied to my texts. But I chose to bite my tongue. Something was clearly bothering her, and I was sure she didn't need my snarky comments on top of everything else.

"I can talk after work, if you want. In fact, I'll be leaving a bit early today because I have an appointment at Sophia's."

Molly couldn't stop a small smile from spreading across her lips. "Trying to get the inside scoop on Tom's murder, I presume?"

I also couldn't resist a grin. "You know me too well."

Molly's smile faded. "I do know you, and I worry about you. I don't know how much you've already heard about this murder, but it sounds like whoever killed Tom was a pretty dangerous person."

I raised an eyebrow at Molly. "You think? I'd have to say that any murderer is a dangerous person. I don't think this case is any more dangerous than any of the other cases I've worked on."

"I'm not so sure about that," Molly said. "Did you hear that someone actually changed the clues on Belinda's scavenger hunt?"

Despite telling myself that I wasn't going to spend any time talking to Molly right now, I couldn't resist hearing more about what she knew. "You heard that too? I was at the scene of the murder when Belinda arrived, and she was ranting that someone had changed the clues. But Ruby was with her at the police station last night, and apparently Belinda never mentioned the changing clues to Ruby. That seems strange, doesn't it?"

Molly narrowed her eyes at me, then glanced around to see whether anyone was paying attention to us. Most people were too busy talking to friends or looking at the menu board to care about our conversation, but Molly lowered her voice anyway.

"You're not suggesting that Belinda had something to do with the murder, are you?"

I lowered my voice as well. "You do know me too well. You know exactly what I'm thinking, don't you? But can you blame me for thinking it? It just seems odd to me that Belinda would claim that someone had changed the clues, but then not even mention it to her best friend."

Molly glanced over at Ruby, looking surprised. Then she glanced back at me. "You really think Belinda and Ruby are best friends? Ruby hasn't even been in Sunshine Springs that long."

I shrugged. "So what? You and I became best friends in a matter of days when I first moved here. And Belinda was probably looking for a friend who wasn't going to judge her for everything that happened with her ex-husband. It can't be easy to go through a divorce in a small town like this, where everyone gossips about you and has their opinion on what you did right and what you did wrong. But Ruby wasn't around when Belinda and Frank broke up, so Ruby has no reason to care about the breakup."

"True," Molly said slowly. "Well, anyway, I think you're reading too much into things. Belinda was probably just overwhelmed by everything that happened yesterday."

"I thought the same thing," I admitted. "But you know how it goes. I have to investigate every potential clue."

I expected Molly to laugh again, but instead she only shook her head. "I wish you wouldn't, Izzy. I really do think this murderer is more dangerous than the others. From what I heard, whoever killed Tom put a lot of effort into changing the clues on the scavenger hunt to lead Tom astray. This murder was incredibly premeditated, and I have a feeling that whoever did it is smart. They're not going to want to get caught, and I'm sure they'll take whatever steps necessary to make sure that they don't—including stopping anyone who tries to track them down."

I felt my annoyance growing. "What's with you today?" I asked Molly. "Usually you're the one cheering me on as I solve these cases. Are you telling me that you're now going to side with Mitch and Theo and everyone else who tells me that I shouldn't be solving murder cases? I thought you were my ride or die chick."

I turned my attention to the milk frother, partially because I really did need to get this latte made, and partially because I was too angry to look at Molly right now. If she cared so much about me, then why hadn't she bothered to check in on me last night? She must have heard about what had happened with Tom, and that I had been there. Yet she hadn't even bothered to check in and see how I was holding up after such an eventful day. And now here she was, trying to tell me that she didn't want me to play detective.

"I am your ride or die," Molly said with a sigh. "It's just that I'd rather not actually die, and I'd rather you didn't die, either. You've solved quite a few murders in the last few months, and I fully admit that you have a talent for sleuthing. But do you have to take on every case that comes along?"

I slammed the mug of espresso I was working on down a little too hard and glared at Molly. I told myself not to say anything that I would regret. After all, Molly was my best friend, and she truly did care for me. I was also running on two hours of sleep, and in my fog of exhaustion I was liable to say something I would regret. But I wasn't in the mood to have this conversation right now, especially not with Molly.

"I'm a big girl, and I can take care of myself. Besides, I wasn't kidding when I said the café is busy. So if all you want to do is lecture me about not doing anything dangerous, then perhaps you should save this conversation for after I'm done with work."

Molly looked like she was about to protest, and even opened her mouth to speak. But then, she closed her mouth once again and set her jaw in a hard line. She glanced at the line of people waiting for pie, then looked back at me. "Fine. I don't want to interrupt you when your café is busy. But I do really need to speak with you, so I'll try to come by Sophia's Snips this afternoon. What time is your appointment?"

"Four," I said, once again looking down at the milk frother instead of at Molly.

"Alright. I'll probably be a bit late, because I have quite a bit to do at the library. But I'll try to be there before you're done. Maybe we could even go grab some ice cream?"

Molly's voice sounded so hopeful that it softened my anger toward her a bit, but not entirely.

"Great," I said in a clipped tone. "I'll see you then." Then, almost as an afterthought, I asked, "Would you like some coffee or pie?"

I always offered Molly free coffee and pie when she was in my café, and even though I was annoyed with her right now, I figured I should continue that trend. She was still my best friend, even if she was driving me crazy at the moment.

But Molly was shaking her head no. "I'll have to pass. I'm actually running late to get to the library. We'll have a busy day there today, too, although of course not as busy as you'll be here. Nothing compares to this." She gestured toward the line and laughed. "I just wanted to see if I might catch you before things here got too crazy, but I should have known I was too late. I'll see you this afternoon."

Before I even had time to reply, Molly had turned to rush out of the café. With a sigh, I turned back to my work. But I couldn't help feeling frustrated. I had thought that once I finally had an employee, that life would slow down and I would have more time to spend with Grams and my friends. But if anything, I felt that life had gotten crazier over the last week. It was probably all just in my imagination, but it did seem that I was working just as hard as ever. On top of that, I now had another murder case weighing on my mind at the same time that my best friend had apparently decided that I needed to be lectured about safety.

Things were a bit of a mess.

My frown deepened as I mulled over everything Molly had said. I didn't see why the fact that Tom's murderer had planned everything so carefully in advance made him or her so much more dangerous than any other murderer I'd chased down. All of the murders I'd dealt with had been premeditated. Why was Molly suddenly so worried about my safety? She was acting strange right now, but I didn't have time to worry too much about it at the moment. The café was busier than ever, and Ruby needed my help.

For the next several hours, I focused completely on making drinks and serving pie. As the day wore on, customers went from wanting coffee drinks to wanting wine, and from wanting non-boozy pies to wanting the full, booze-filled versions of my pies. As expected, the lemon vodka pies flew off the shelves. It looked like we might have finally made enough to not sell out for the day, but it was going to be close.

I tried not to think about my worries over Tom's murder and Molly's strange behavior. Instead I focused on selling as much pie as possible. When 3 p.m. came, I asked Ruby if she would mind if I left her to run the shop by herself. As I expected, she seemed thrilled at the idea. She wanted the opportunity to prove herself, and I resisted the urge to remind her to turn off the coffee machine today. I wanted to see what she could do on her own, without nagging reminders from me. She seemed smart and capable, and I didn't want to judge her based on how she had performed last night—not when the night had been so unusual and dramatic.

Ruby practically shooed me out the door, telling me to relax and have fun. She'd had zero hours of sleep the night before, which was even less than my measly two hours of sleep. But she still seemed more awake than me. I chalked it up to the fact that she was probably a decade younger than me, and told her to feel free to drink as much espresso as she needed. Then I left the café in a hurry.

I wanted to stop at the grocery store on the way to Sophia's and pick up a few things. I wasn't sure how well Sophia would take it if I showed up with a bag of food, but I was worried that she wasn't eating enough. I hoped that she would be grateful for a few things to put in her pantry, instead of offended that I'd thought it necessary to buy food for her.

And I hoped that I would learn more about what had happened on that fateful afternoon that Tom had died. Even though Sophia was currently acting a bit strange, I knew that her hair salon would still be the best place to get information about this murder case.

And I didn't care who told me that it was too dangerous to get involved: I was going to get information, and I was going to help solve this case.

I set my face in a determined line as I left the Drunken Pie Café. Time to chase down some clues.

CHAPTER SIX

I made my way quickly through the grocery store, loading up a hand basket with an assortment of bread, cheese, salami, and fruit. I had plenty of time until my appointment, and yet somehow I still felt rushed. The events of the last twenty-four hours had given me a sense of urgency, and I felt that the sooner I could get to the hair salon and see whether anyone had news on Tom's murder, the better.

I was just about to go pay when I decided to add a bottle of wine to my purchases. Sophia seemed like she could use a chance to kick back and relax, and a bottle of wine from the local winery seemed like just the thing. I hurried to the wine aisle of the grocery store, and stopped in surprise when I rounded the corner and saw who was standing there.

"Theo! What are you doing here? I would think that if you wanted to buy wine, you could get it directly from your winery instead of needing to purchase it from the grocery store."

Theo Russo looked up, and smiled when he saw me. His handsome, dark features and twinkling eyes made my stomach flip-flop a bit—although I would never admit that to him. He had already tried to convince me to date him, and I had declined. I just wasn't ready for a man in my life. I was still recovering from a heartbreaking divorce, and besides, my café kept me quite busy. I barely had time to hang out with Molly, let alone time to go on dates. Theo seemed to have accepted this, but that didn't stop him from flirting when he happened to run across me.

"Of course I can get wine from the winery anytime I want," he said. "But sometimes when I'm in the grocery store I can't help stopping by the wine aisles to see my products on display. You'd think that it would eventually get old, but I still haven't gotten tired of seeing wine from my family's winery on the shelves. Besides, you never know when you might run into a pretty lady in the wine aisle of the grocery store."

He wiggled his eyebrows at me, and my heart did another flip-flop. But I refused to let him see that he was affecting me. Instead, I rolled my eyes at him and gestured toward my basket of food.

"I'm just picking up a few things for Sophia. She's been a little distraught since Tom's murder happened, and I thought maybe some food would cheer her up."

I didn't explain to Theo just how distraught Sophia actually was. I figured that she was going through a rough time, and there was no need to broadcast the extent of that roughness to everyone. But Theo's expression sobered, and I got the feeling that he might have a clue as to just how rough things were.

"Mitch told me that she was downright hysterical after what happened," Theo said. "Not that anyone can blame her for that. I'm sure it's quite upsetting to see a dead body."

"You're telling me. I wasn't too pleased myself about seeing Tom in that condition."

Theo raised an eyebrow. "So you actually saw the body, then? Mitch told me you were there, but I didn't know how much you had seen."

"Yes, I was there, and I saw far more than I wanted to. I don't know who would do such a thing, but…"

I trailed off, but Theo knew exactly what I was intending to say. "But you're determined to find out, aren't you?"

I shrugged sheepishly in response. "I can't help it if these murder cases keep dropping in my lap. And you have to admit that I'm a good detective."

Theo shook his head. "You're smart, Izzy, and that makes you a good detective. I'm not going to argue with that. But I really wish you'd leave this case alone. I think this is an especially dangerous case."

I let out an exasperated sigh. "Everyone keeps saying that. Molly said the same thing, but I don't see how this is any more dangerous than any other case."

It was Theo's turn to sigh. "All of these cases are dangerous, true. You're dealing with people who think it's okay to actually take someone's life. But whoever this criminal is, they sound especially nasty, and I wish you'd stick to baking pies instead of chasing down murderers. This criminal planned things out in detail, and was quite violent in the way he or she took out Tom. I'd rather not see you get mixed up in that sort of thing."

As Theo spoke, he reached out and put his hand on my upper arm. When I looked up and met his gaze, I couldn't quite ignore the electricity that seemed to crackle in the air between us. Quickly, I looked down.

Theo was handsome, smart, and kind. Not to mention he was fabulously wealthy as the owner of the Sunshine Springs Winery. But again, I wasn't looking for a man right now, no matter how great that man was. I took a step backward, worried that my cheeks were red. I could feel them heating up with a mixture of longing and embarrassment.

"I'll be careful," I said quickly. "I always am."

Theo raised an eyebrow at me. "I'm not so sure about that. I've seen you do some pretty reckless things in the pursuit of a case."

"Okay, perhaps I've done a few things that weren't exactly the smartest. But everything has always turned out okay."

"What if it doesn't this time?" Theo asked. "Don't you think you should quit while you're ahead?"

I shrugged. "Nope. I think I should keep working on cases. I'm good at it, and Mitch appreciates my help, whether he admits to it or not."

Theo shook his head. "Mitch wishes that you would stay safe. You know that."

"I'll stay safe," I insisted again. "Besides, this is exactly my kind of case. It's twisty and complicated, and I can really help Mitch. Did you know that whoever killed Tom apparently changed the clues on the scavenger hunt Belinda had set up?"

"Yes, I knew that. That's why I said this murderer is smart and dangerous. They put a lot of thought and work into this."

I ignored Theo's comment about the murderer being dangerous, and plowed ahead with my suspicions of Belinda. I lowered my voice slightly as I spoke—I didn't know who else might be in the grocery store, and Belinda was local. Some people might not take kindly to my having suspicions of a local, no matter how much that local had fallen out of favor at the moment.

"I think Belinda might have made up that story about the changed clues to avoid being blamed herself."

Theo frowned at me. "I'm not so sure about that. I know that Mitch reviewed the scavenger hunt clues that Belinda had, and compared them to the clues that were found on Tom when he died. It does appear as though the clues had been changed, so there might be some validity to what Belinda was saying. I don't think it was Belinda that changed them. In fact, she claims that someone called her to say Tom was in danger near those lemon trees right around the time he died. Her phone records confirmed that she received a call from an untraceable number at or around the time of Tom's death. Mitch thinks that whoever killed Tom was trying to get Belinda to show up at the scene of the crime so that she would be blamed."

I felt my heart beating with excitement. Theo's brow was furrowed, and he was thinking so deeply about the case that he didn't realize that he was giving me information that Mitch probably would have preferred he kept to himself. Mitch didn't like it when anyone shared information on an ongoing case, especially when they were sharing that information with me. But Theo often talked to me about cases. He couldn't resist a conversation with me, and Mitch couldn't resist telling Theo what was going on, since Theo and Mitch were best friends. I hoped that Theo would continue to discuss the case with me now, and I cocked my head quizzically in his direction.

"What if Belinda made up that story and made sure that she received a phone call to cast blame off of her?" I asked. "I know that she didn't say anything about the changed clues to Ruby, and Ruby was with her at the police station last night. Don't you think that Belinda would have told Ruby about the changed clues if it was really true?"

"Maybe, maybe not. From what Mitch tells me, Belinda was quite incoherent last night. Whether that was an act or not, who knows. But it's certainly feasible that she just didn't mention something because she was too overwhelmed by everything to think straight."

"So is Mitch considering her a suspect or not?" I asked.

At that moment, Theo seemed to realize that he was talking too much. He narrowed his eyes at me, and shook his head. "I shouldn't be talking to you about this. You know that."

"Oh, come on. You know I'm going to hear everything through the gossip mill, anyway."

Theo shrugged. "Probably. But you shouldn't be hearing it from me. You know Mitch would have my head if he knew I was divulging this information to you."

I sighed. It looked like my few minutes of picking Theo's brain had come to an end. Now that he'd realized he was talking too much, I knew it would be useless to try to get him to continue talking. I made a pouty face at him.

"Fine. I'll go through the gossip mill, then. Speaking of which, I should head over to Sophia's Snips. If I don't get going, I'm going to be late for my appointment."

Theo shrugged. "Alright. I'm sure you're going to hear everything that's going on while you're there, and it's only going to whet your appetite for more. Just please, be careful. It would kill me if anything happened to you."

"I'll do my best," I said, once again trying not to make it obvious that Theo's concern made my heart do funny flip-flops in my chest. I mumbled goodbye, and made my way to the checkout as quickly as I could.

I didn't need to be distracted by Theo and his good looks right now. I had a murder to solve.

And yet, as I left the grocery store a few minutes later, I couldn't resist looking behind me to see if I could catch one last glimpse of Theo. He was standing not too far from the lane where I had just checked out, watching me with an intense gaze.

I swallowed hard, trying to stuff down my feelings, and hurried out of the grocery store without another look back.

CHAPTER SEVEN

When I pulled into Sophia's Snips Hair Salon and Spa, I wasn't surprised to see that the parking lot was full. Any time any major, gossip-worthy event happened, everyone wanted to be at Sophia's Snips. It was the best place to hear all the latest news. I also wasn't surprised to see Grams' car there. I hadn't had a chance to talk to her and see when I could pick up Sprinkles, but I should have known she'd be there. I couldn't hold back a grin, wondering what bright, neon color Sprinkles' toenails would be painted today.

I parked in the last available parking spot, then grabbed my bag of goodies for Sophia and made my way toward the salon's frosted glass front door. To my surprise, as I reached for the door handle, the door flew open and Sheriff Mitch himself came barreling out. He seemed distracted, and almost bowled me over before realizing that I was standing right in front of him.

"Izzy! I'm sorry. I didn't see you there."

"That's alright," I said quickly as I shifted my bag of groceries in my arms. "But what are you doing here? Something tells me that you're not here to get your nails done."

Ordinarily, Mitch would have laughed at a joke like that. But today, he didn't seem to be in a laughing mood. He cracked his knuckles, and ran his fingers through his hair in a distracted manner.

"I might as well tell you, since I'm sure you'll hear as soon as you head into the salon. I came to talk to Sophia about Tom's murder. She's officially a person of interest in the case, so I had to ask her not to leave town. It's a formality, of course. I doubt she was planning on going anywhere outside of Sunshine Springs, but I was obligated to let her know."

My jaw dropped. "Are you serious? Sophia is a person of interest? Do you really think she had something to do with Tom's death?"

"Honestly? I don't think it was her. But she was the first one on the scene as far as we know, and she can't explain to us what she was actually doing out there. That puts a cloud of suspicion over her, and I had no choice but to consider her a suspect."

I swallowed hard, realizing that I had also been at the scene of the crime not long after the murder happened. "I hope you're not going to consider me a suspect, too."

I had already been on the suspect list for another murder in Sunshine Springs. That had been when I first arrived in town, and a woman had dropped dead right in front of my café. I'd been cleared of that murder, but being unjustly accused of murder had not been pleasant, to say the least. I had no desire to repeat that experience.

Despite the fact that he was obviously stressed out, I saw a hint of amusement in Mitch's eyes. "You're not currently a suspect, since Sophia herself verified for us that you and your grandmother arrived at the scene after her, and that Tom was already dead at that time. But if you'd like to join the fun, I can add you to the suspect list."

I groaned. "No, thank you. I'll pass on that one."

"Good choice. I don't think you have it in you to kill someone, anyway. I don't think Sophia has it in her, either. But, like I said, I don't have a choice but to consider her a suspect. I have to be thorough in my investigations. I checked out Frank, too, since he might have had motive to kill Tom. But Frank has a solid alibi, so in this case the murder wasn't committed by a jealous ex-husband." Mitch stopped and gave me a sharp look. "Whoever did this was extremely dangerous. You better be staying out of things."

I squinted at Mitch. "Everyone keeps saying that whoever did this was extremely dangerous. But isn't that true of all murderers? I don't see how this is any more dangerous than any other case I've dealt with."

Mitch grunted in annoyance and cracked his knuckles again. "I knew it. You're already thinking of yourself as a detective on this case, aren't you?"

"Maybe," I said noncommittally.

"That's a yes if I ever heard one. Listen, Izzy. Tom died from a blow to the back of the head. Whoever killed him used a sharp object at close range, and that takes a really sick kind of person. With the other murder cases you've been involved with, the killers used poison or a gun. That doesn't require being at close range to kill, so it's a bit more impersonal and removed. But killing someone at close range by stabbing them in the back of the head? That's pretty up close and personal. It takes an especially sick individual to do something like that. It takes someone willing to be extra evil. Please, I'm begging you: For once could you just leave the detective work to the real detectives and stay out of danger?"

I merely shrugged. I wasn't scared of this murderer any more than any other murderer, and the thrill of the chase was too much for me to resist. There was no way I was going to promise Mitch to stay out of things.

Mitch knew exactly what my silence meant, and let out a long sigh. "I was afraid of that. If you'll excuse me, then, I have a lot of work to do. I see that the only way I'm going to get you to leave this case alone is to solve it myself before you do. I just hope I can find the murderer and lock them away before they hurt you or someone else. But especially you. You know I care deeply about you, Izzy."

Mitch gave me a long, hard look, and I once again felt my heart doing a little flip-flop. Mitch was just as handsome as Theo, and was also interested in me. True, sometimes it drove me crazy the way Mitch wanted to boss me around and told me not to investigate things. But I knew that the reason he was always so insistent that I leave these cases alone was that he cared about me deep down. He might have been overprotective, but he was overprotective because he didn't want to see me get hurt. Could I really fault him for that?

And even though he didn't like my working on these cases, I liked feeling like I was part of the team with him. Okay, I wasn't an official part of his team. But that didn't matter. I enjoyed working alongside him to bring criminals to justice. It brought me a great deal of joy and pride when I could help Mitch, and I'd be lying if I said I didn't crave his approval at least a little bit. When he said or did something that made it obvious that he cared about me, I couldn't help but swoon a bit. I just hoped it wasn't obvious to him that I was swooning.

I felt my cheeks heating up, and I mentally chided myself. I needed to get a grip. In the space of the last half hour, I'd let myself get giddy about both Theo and Mitch. But I wasn't interested in either of them, or in any other man for that matter. I needed to get over myself and get into the salon so I could hear what everyone else knew about Tom's murder. Mitch's declaration that he was going to solve this quickly felt like a challenge to me. It was all I could do to keep from winking at him and saying, "Challenge accepted."

I kept these sentiments to myself, but inwardly I was already thinking about how I could beat Mitch to figuring out who had killed Tom. Mitch had an advantage over me, since he had access to all of the evidence in the case. But I was determined, and that counted for a lot. I'd gotten a lot of things in my life just by being determined and not giving up. Why should this be any different? There was no reason I couldn't be the first to solve this case, with a little bit of hard work.

Of course, I didn't say anything to Mitch about this. Instead, I smiled and said, "Well, don't let me keep you from your work. I've got a hair appointment to get to."

I flashed Mitch a winning smile, and before he could say anything else, I ducked inside the salon. To my shock, Sophia was sitting in one of her salon chairs in tears. She was surrounded by several of the local woman, Grams among them. Everyone looked distraught, even Sprinkles, who was sitting next to Grams and only managed a few weak thumps of his tail when he saw me.

For a moment, all I could do was stare. It had been shocking enough to see Sophia upset at her home yesterday. But the fact that she was this upset in the middle of her salon took things to a whole new level. Sophia had always been the type to laugh stuff off, and the Sophia I knew would have laughed off even a murder accusation.

Unless, perhaps, that murder accusation was grounded in truth?

I shuddered, and tried to swallow back the sudden, sick sensation that filled me. Was it possible that Sophia was not as nice and innocent as we all thought she was?

At that moment, Sophia looked up at me with tear-filled eyes, and seemed to realize for the first time that I had entered the salon.

"Izzy, dear," she said in a shaky voice. "I'm really sorry but I don't think I can cut your hair today. I've just had the most shocking news. Mitch thinks that I killed Tom! Can you believe it? He actually told me that I'm a suspect in the case. I'm so upset that my hands are shaking, so I don't think it's a good idea for me to cut hair right now."

Tears spilled over onto her cheeks as she spoke, and I felt a rush of sympathy. I felt badly that I'd thought for even a moment that her distress was a sign of guilt. Even though Sophia had always been bubbly and strong, and had let bad things roll off her back, this was a bit more serious than most normal bad days. She had every right to be upset, and I went over to pat her shoulder and reassure her that I wasn't upset about the haircut. Really, she probably knew as well as I did that I hadn't made the appointment because I wanted a haircut so badly. I mostly wanted to know what was going on with the murder case, and being here now allowed me to hear the latest news whether I was actually getting my hair cut or not. I held out the bag of food to her with an empathetic smile on my face.

"Don't worry about the haircut. I'll reschedule for another time. And look, I brought you some food. I know you've been busy and overwhelmed, and I thought you might appreciate a little care package of goodies."

Sophia looked up at me and then at the bag, and more tears flowed over onto her cheeks. "That was so thoughtful of you. I could definitely use a glass of that wine. I've never been so upset in my life."

"Don't worry," I said soothingly, already reaching to pull out the bottle of wine to open it for her. "Trust me. I know how distressing it is to be accused of murder. But I promise you that everything works out in the end." And then, in a sudden fit of heroism, I stood straighter and declared, "And besides, I'm going to help solve this case. I promise you: I'm going to figure out who really killed Tom, and clear your name. Everyone knows I'm a good detective. I'll figure this out. Don't you worry."

But instead of looking reassured by this, Sophia only looked more distressed.

"It's hopeless," she exclaimed as she dissolved into all-out sobbing. How is anyone ever going to believe that it wasn't me who killed Tom when it was a pair of scissors from my hair salon that killed him?"

I frowned, and looked at the faces of Grams and the other ladies to see whether they were as shocked as I was by this news. But they must have already known, because they were all shaking their heads sadly. Even Sprinkles looked forlorn, as though he understood that today Sophia's Snips wasn't the same happy place that it usually was.

"Is that true?" I asked, directing my question to Grams.

Grams shrugged and nodded. "According to Mitch it's true. When he came in just now to talk to Sophia, he said that the murder weapon was scissors from the salon. That, combined with the fact that Sophia was at the scene of the crime, makes her look guilty."

Sophia started sobbing harder, and Grams patted her arm. "I'm not saying I believe that you're guilty, Sophia. I'm just saying that that's why Mitch had to add you to the suspect list. I'm sure this will get sorted out, especially if Izzy's going to work on the case. You know she's the best detective around."

I couldn't help but stand a little straighter at the pride that I heard in Grams' voice. It made me feel good to know how much Grams believed in me.

"It's true," I said to Sophia. "I'm a good detective. I'll figure this out." Then I looked back at Grams. "Did Mitch say whether they fingerprinted the scissors? Surely if they did then they would have found prints on them besides Sophia's?"

But Grams was shaking her head. "Sophia's prints were on the scissors, but that doesn't mean anything. Sophia uses her scissors every day, so of course her prints would be on them. All Tom's murderer would have had to do was use gloves to avoid getting their own prints on the scissors, and it would look like Sophia was the murderer."

I nodded. That made sense. If the murderer had been careful enough to change all of the clues for the scavenger hunt, and to call Belinda to get Belinda out to the murder scene, then of course they would have been smart enough not to leave fingerprints on the murder weapon.

Assuming, of course, that Sophia really was innocent. I stared at her for a moment, watching as she sobbed into her hands. She had been acting strangely, but there was no way she was actually the murderer, was there? Surely, she was just overwhelmed by everything going on.

I frowned as I mulled things over. Neither Belinda nor Sophia really seemed like the type to kill, but could I really be certain? There was evidence against both of them, and Sophia had seemed to dislike Tom quite strongly. But still, that dislike wasn't strong enough to make her kill him, was it?

I tried to think of what other information Sophia might have that would be helpful, and I couldn't stop wondering why she had been at the scene of the crime in the first place. I decided to ask her. Maybe if she could explain that further, then I might understand things better.

"Can you tell me why you were there by the lemon grove?" I asked in a gentle voice. "If we can establish that you had a legitimate reason for being there, that will help your case."

I expected these words to give Sophia some hope, but they seemed to have the opposite effect. Almost immediately, she started sobbing harder. Then, she became angry.

"Why does it matter why I was there?" she asked in a furious tone. "It's a free country. I have every right to be driving by the lemon grove if I want to! The fact that I was there doesn't prove anything. Why can't anyone see that?"

I was taken aback by this angry outburst, and the sick feeling of suspicion I felt only grew stronger. But I swallowed that suspicion back for the moment, and continued to act sympathetic toward Sophia.

"Of course it's a free country," I said soothingly. "But unfortunately, being near the murder casts you in a bad light. Showing that you were there for a legitimate reason would help clear your name."

"I don't have to explain myself to anyone!" Sophia yelled, suddenly jumping up from the chair and sending the ladies surrounding her rushing backward to avoid her flailing arms. "Do you hear me? I don't have to explain myself to anyone!"

Before anyone could say anything else, Sophia burst into sobs again and took off running to the back room. We all stood there, stunned. One of the women started to head after Sophia, but Grams put a hand on the woman's arm to stop her.

"Let her go," Grams said. "I think she just needs some time alone."

The woman nodded, but then we all stood awkwardly for a few moments looking around at each other. No one said it, but I could tell that a few people were thinking it: if Sophia had nothing to hide, then why was she so upset when asked why she'd been at the lemon grove?

I hated to admit it, especially because I'd always liked Sophia so much, but she was starting to move to the top of my suspect list. Still, things didn't make sense. Sophia didn't strike me as the murdering type, and as far as I could see she didn't have a strong motive to get rid of Tom.

I was missing something here, but I wasn't going to be getting any more information from Sophia—at least not today. I would have to figure out another way to find out why Sophia had been near Tom the day he died, and whether her reasons were somehow connected to his death. I shivered again, and started to turn toward the door.

"I should go," I said as I gestured toward Sprinkles to follow me. "Clearly, I'm not getting a haircut today, so there's no point in my hanging around here."

Just as I turned toward the front door, it opened and Molly walked in. In the midst of all the excitement, I had forgotten that my best friend was supposed to meet me here today. When Molly stepped inside and took one look at the somber faces in the room, she instantly knew that something was wrong.

"What's going on here?" she asked.

I sighed. "It's a long story. But let's just say that Sophia isn't in the mood to cut my hair today."

Molly raised one eyebrow. "Interesting...I don't suppose I could convince you to go for ice cream, then, like I suggested earlier?"

I smiled wearily. "Ice cream sounds great. I have a lot to tell you, and doing it over a delicious dessert sounds a lot more enjoyable than awkwardly sitting around here."

I followed Molly out the front door without another look back, thinking how strange this day had been. And it only felt stranger when Molly turned to look at me with uneasy eyes and said, "I have a lot to tell you, too."

My exhaustion was growing greater by the moment, but I had a feeling it was going to be a while yet before I made it to bed.

CHAPTER EIGHT

The line at the ice-cream parlor on Main Street was about as long as the line at my café had been earlier. In the midst of this heat wave, it seemed that boozy pie and ice cream were equally as popular.

Molly and I made small talk as we waited. The line didn't seem like the best place to discuss a murder case, and whatever it was that Molly wanted to tell me was apparently not something she wanted to discuss in the middle of the line, either. There were too many people around, and we both seemed to mutually agree that we would just make small talk until we got our ice cream and could sit in a more secluded spot.

The sweet, sugary smell of waffle cones and ice cream made my mouth water, and I ordered myself an extra large scoop of cake batter ice cream in a sprinkle covered waffle cone. The ice-cream parlor had an outdoor patio that stretched across the sidewalk all the way up to the edge of the street, and Molly and I sat outside in a far corner since Sprinkles was with us.

As we sat down, Sprinkles looked up at me and whined, but I shook my head at him. "No ice cream for you today, boy. You can't fool me. You've been with Grams all day, and I know how she is. She's been pumping you full of sugar, I'm sure. You know too much sugar will make you sick."

Sprinkles didn't even try to protest. Instead, with a resigned sigh, he flopped down onto the ground next to me.

Molly couldn't help but laugh. "I can't believe how much your grandmother spoils that dog. Can you imagine if you ever have actual human babies? She'll spoil them like crazy!"

I groaned. "I'm sure any human babies I have will be ridiculously spoiled. But it doesn't seem I'll have to worry about that. My love life is nonexistent at the moment, and I'm pretty sure the saying goes 'first comes love, then comes marriage, then come the babies.'"

Molly crossed her arms. "You have no love life because you don't want one. You've had plenty of men interested in you."

I squirmed uncomfortably in my seat. "They're not really interested in me," I joked. "They just want to be with someone who will bake them boozy pie anytime they want."

I tried to laugh, but Molly didn't laugh with me. Instead, her face grew serious, and she opened her mouth to speak. "Yeah, well, about that—"

From the look on her face, I could tell that Molly had been about to tell me something important. Perhaps it was whatever important thing she'd been trying to tell me all day. But before she could get any more words out, a familiar voice was calling out my name.

"Izzy! I thought you were going to get your hair done?"

I looked over to see Ruby approaching us. Self-consciously, I reached up and touched the frizzy mess of a bun that my hair was still styled in. After a nearly sleepless night, I hadn't had the energy to do much with my hair, especially when I was planning to go get it done professionally that afternoon anyway. I could only imagine how ridiculous it must look right now, but I looked over at Ruby and shrugged.

"Sophia had to cancel my appointment. She's had a…bit of a rough day."

For some reason, I didn't want to say anything to Ruby about how Sophia had suddenly become an official person of interest. Ruby would hear about that soon enough, but I didn't want to be the one to tell her and then have to answer all the questions she was sure to have.

But apparently, Ruby had already heard that Sophia was a person of interest, and just the mention of Sophia was enough to set Ruby off. Her face darkened, and she let out a snarl. "Good. Sophia should be having a rough day. I'm glad to hear that Mitch is at least trying to go after someone who actually might have killed Tom instead of focusing all of his attention needlessly on Belinda."

Something about Ruby's ranting about Mitch made me angry.

Sure, Mitch could get overzealous about certain things. But he was a good detective, and he was trying his best. Ruby was barely more than an outsider in Sunshine Springs at this point. Who did she think she was, slamming Mitch? Didn't she know that he was a good friend of mine?

"Mitch is just doing his job," I said in an even voice. "He has to cover all his bases."

Ruby snorted. "If he wants to cover all his bases, then all he needs to do is look at Sophia. It's obvious to anyone that she hated Tom. If Mitch knows what's good for him, he'll accuse her and get her locked away before she hurts someone else. Didn't you hear that it was her scissors used to kill Tom? The truth is obvious!"

I raised my eyebrows in surprise. "Wow. News travels fast in this town."

As far as I knew, no one had known that the murder weapon came from Sophia's Snips until Mitch went to the salon to talk to Sophia. That didn't give much time for the news to spread between then and now, but I shouldn't have been that surprised. The Sunshine Springs gossip train never ceased to amaze me with its speed, and besides, I realized that I didn't actually know for sure that no one else had known before Mitch went to the salon. There was always a possibility that Scott had heard something while making package deliveries to the police station. Whatever the case, I wasn't in the mood to discuss this with Ruby, so I tried to change the subject.

"Well, Mitch is very capable. I'm sure he'll have this all taken care of in no time. Since you're here, though, how was the rest of the day at the café? Busy?"

Ruby shook her head. "Not really. Apparently, everyone comes for ice cream in the afternoon instead of boozy pie these days. After you left, the crowds dwindled pretty quickly. But don't worry. I'm sure the sales for the day overall were still good, since the morning was so crazy busy."

"Huh," I said. "Maybe this is what it looks like when we reach the tail end of the tourist season."

This was my first year in Sunshine Springs, so I didn't really know what to expect yet. The tourist season was slowly winding down, and maybe that meant that the afternoons were going to start being less busy. I glanced at my watch, and realized that it was only about twenty minutes past the time when the Drunken Pie Café normally closed. Things must have been really slow for Ruby to have already finished up closing duties and still have had time to walk over here to the ice-cream parlor. Or perhaps Ruby had worked too quickly and had once again missed things while closing up the café. I half-expected to find the espresso machine still on when I arrived to bake pies the next morning.

Ruby let out a long sigh, drawing me back to the present moment.

"I'm sorry if I came across as rude. I know Mitch is your friend, and I don't want to say bad things about him. It's just that I know Belinda is innocent, and it's frustrating to see her going through all of this." Ruby shook her head side to side sadly. "I don't know Sophia that well, but I know the evidence points to her much more than it does to Belinda. But anyway, I just hope that the true murderer is caught soon so that we can all relax a bit and try to get back to our normal lives. Of course, it's going to be hard for Belinda to do that. She just lost the love of her life."

Ruby shook her head sadly again, her ponytail bouncing against her shoulders as she did. In that moment, I couldn't help being annoyed with Ruby. I knew that she probably meant well, and I knew she was only saying those things because she cared about Belinda. But she was going to step on a lot of toes if she went around accusing Sophia.

I was wary of arguing with her too much, though. I needed her help at the café, so I didn't want to sour our relationship with the debate over Tom's murder. At the end of it all, the true murderer would be found out, and that would be that.

Ruby seemed to sense as much as I did that it was best to drop the subject. She put a bright smile on her face and looked toward the menu of ice-cream flavors that was artfully displayed on a chalkboard stand at the edge of the patio.

"Anyway, enough talk about murders," Ruby said with a wide smile. "I'm here to enjoy some ice cream, just like you ladies."

There was a pause that quickly became awkward when I realized that Ruby was probably expecting me to invite her to sit with us. Despite the frustrations of the last few minutes, I did enjoy Ruby's company, and ordinarily I would have been happy to ask her to sit with Molly and me. But today I had been hoping to discuss the murder case with Molly, and also to hear whatever it was that Molly had to tell me. I had a feeling that neither of those things would be happening if Ruby sat down with us. Still, I didn't see a way to avoid asking Ruby to sit with us without being rude, so I took a deep breath and decided to suck it up and ask her to pull up a chair.

My attempts at being polite were suddenly interrupted, however, when I saw Scott rushing forward across the crowded patio space. His eyes were wide, and he looked like he had news to share.

"Scott?" Molly asked in a surprised tone, apparently just as startled to see him as I was.

"You'll never believe what I just heard," he exclaimed. Instantly, he had the attention of Molly, Ruby, and me. If Scott was excited about something, then you knew it was going to be good. He usually acted pretty stoic about whatever events were going on in town.

"What did you hear?" I demanded, impatient for him to spit it out.

"Somebody set the lemon grove on fire!" he exclaimed. Then, for the space of several heartbeats, the three of us just stared at him.

Ruby found her voice first. "What! Do you mean *the* lemon grove? The same spot where Tom was murdered?"

Scott nodded vigorously. "Yes, *the* lemon grove. I was just at the fire station making a late afternoon delivery, and it was all the firemen were talking about. About an hour earlier, they received a call reporting smoke. By the time they got there, half the grove was up in flames. It's too early to know for sure, but everyone pretty much suspects that the fire was intentional."

My eyes widened as I processed all of this. "It must have been the murderer!" I said, the excitement growing in my voice. "They were probably trying to destroy evidence. Why else would someone set that lemon grove on fire?"

Scott was still nodding. "Yup. There must have been some evidence there that they wanted to cover up. I can't wait to hear what Mitch and the others down at the station are saying about this."

I couldn't wait either. But instead of standing around merely discussing it like Scott, I decided that I was going to take action. I jumped to my feet and grabbed my purse. Sprinkles scrambled up beside me, startled by my sudden movement.

"Izzy?" Molly asked, a hint of suspicion starting to form in her voice. "What are you doing?"

"I need to check on something," I said, then started dashing toward my car before anyone could ask me any more questions. I knew that if I told Molly and Scott what I was doing, they would try to talk me out of it. Nobody wanted me involved in this case, but that was alright. I didn't need anyone's permission, and I wasn't going to stand around waiting for it.

I tossed the remainder of my ice-cream cone in the trash—a sad loss, but holding onto the cone would only slow me down—and I ran toward my car to drive toward the lemon grove.

I could hear Molly calling out behind me, telling me to stop. I knew she had probably quickly figured out what I was doing, but I didn't turn around to talk to her. Not even my best friend could convince me to stop this quest. I wanted to see the lemon grove while the damage from the fire was still fresh. I knew that the person who had set the fire would undoubtedly be long gone. But perhaps they had left some sort of clue behind as to who they were.

Perhaps I could find some evidence that would lead me closer to discovering who had killed Tom Schmidt.

CHAPTER NINE

I drove way too fast toward the grove, my heart pounding with excitement. Sprinkles sat in the passenger seat beside me, barking excitedly the whole drive. At one point, I looked over at him and couldn't help but smile. Perhaps everyone else didn't approve of my detective efforts, but Sprinkles was always down for these adventures.

"I can always count on you, boy," I said, reaching over to rub the short fur behind his ears while I was on a straight, flat stretch of road. Sprinkles barked happily in response, his tail pumping wildly as we raced down the road.

Oddly enough, my own mood was soaring. It had been a long, exhausting day, and I'd be lying if I said I didn't feel the strain with Ruby and in my friendship with Molly. Things were a bit rough in several areas of my life right now. But I would worry about that later. Right now, I had the chance to possibly discover more clues about Tom's murder. The excitement and adrenaline of the moment overcame the exhaustion and worries that tried to plague me.

My excitement faded somewhat, though, when I drove up on the road next to the lemon grove and saw that Mitch was there. I groaned, and slapped my palm to my forehead.

Of course he was here. There was a possible arson case, which was connected to a murder case. Somehow, in my giddy state of exhaustion, it had never occurred to me that I wouldn't be the only one interested in checking out this crime scene.

I knew Mitch would not be pleased to see me showing up here, but it never crossed my mind to turn around. Mitch could be mad at me all he wanted, but I was determined to help with this case.

His back was turned toward me as I approached with Sprinkles, but he must have already seen me and known I was coming. He spoke to me without turning around.

"This is a crime scene, Izzy. You can't just walk all over it and contaminate it."

"I won't. I promise," I said brightly. "I'll stay on this side of the yellow crime scene tape."

That yellow crime scene tape seemed to be everywhere. It had been wrapped around the trees on the outer edges of the grove— well, what was left of the trees anyway. The leaves and lemons were completely gone from most of the trees, and the trunks were all charred and smoldering. A heavy, sulfur-like smell hung in the air, and I wrinkled my nose in disgust.

"Looks like somebody wanted to destroy evidence," I said.

Mitch finally turned around and raised a weary eyebrow in my direction. "Thank you, Captain Obvious."

I winced, but I wasn't going to let his dripping sarcasm deter me. I plowed ahead with my observations. "Don't you think it's a little strange that they burnt the lemon grove now, though? Surely, your detectives have already combed this area for evidence."

"Of course they have. But we were planning on coming out here again this afternoon to try to comb for anything that might provide DNA evidence. Originally we had a few DNA samples we found that we thought might have been from the killer. But when we analyzed things, much of the evidence was too contaminated to give us any clear conclusions. And anything that wasn't too contaminated turned out to be from Tom, which obviously doesn't help us in figuring out who killed him. I thought it was a long shot, but I was planning to come through here another time to see what else we could find. Something tells me that we would have found something interesting. Otherwise, why would someone have set this lemon grove on fire?"

"That makes sense," I said slowly. "But there's just one problem."

"What's that?" Mitch asked, although he didn't seem that interested in what I was saying. He looked like he was off in another world, distracted and worried. I decided to keep talking, anyway.

"I just don't understand how the killer would have known you were coming out here today. I'm guessing that you didn't put a billboard up on Main Street outlining your plan, so how did they know to come burn things today?"

Mitch cracked his knuckles. "Yeah, I thought about that. It doesn't make sense to me either. The only people I told were my staff. And I made sure that no one else was at the station to overhear when we were talking about it. Your friend Scott wasn't delivering packages, so I know he didn't hear and blab it all over town."

"Hey, don't act like it's somehow my fault that Scott's such a gossip. He's your friend, too."

Mitch cracked a smile. "True. But you hang out with him more than you hang out with me. That hurts a guy's ego, you know."

Mitch looked up at me and managed to smile. I put my hands on my hips and shook a finger at him.

"Maybe if you didn't always tell me to stay out of things, then I would hang out with you more. You and Theo are both always getting onto me like you're my parents and can tell me what to do."

Mitch's face turned serious once again. "I just don't want you to get hurt. In fact, you shouldn't be here. What if the killer is watching, and sees that you're involved? I don't want them to hurt you."

I resisted the urge to roll my eyes again. "No one's going to hurt me. And how would anyone be watching? You can see pretty far in every direction out here, especially now that these trees are burnt to a crisp."

Mitch merely shrugged, apparently too tired to argue with me anymore. When he spoke again, he almost sounded like he was talking to himself, even though he was speaking out loud. "Well, whoever this killer is, they seem to have eyes and ears everywhere. Somehow, they knew we were coming out here today. I don't know what the explanation is for that. I can't imagine that there's someone on the inside at the police station working with the killer. All of my employees are solid. I'd stake my life on it."

"But then how did someone know that they needed to bring this lemon grove down?" I mused.

Mitch shrugged again, looking more tired than I'd ever seen him. I got the feeling that he hadn't gotten much more sleep the night before than I had. He gave me another weary look, then made a shooing motion with his hands in my direction. "Come on, Izzy. Get out of here. There's nothing to see anyway, and I'd feel better if you went back into town where it's safe."

For a moment, I thought about protesting and telling him that he had no proof that town was any safer than here. For all we knew, the killer was walking around on Main Street in Sunshine Springs right now.

Heck, the killer might be Belinda or Sophia. Not that I *really* thought that, but I couldn't rule it out either. All I knew for sure was that the sooner the killer was caught, the safer everyone would be. And I wanted to help catch the killer.

But the look of exhaustion on Mitch's face made me decide to leave without a fight. Mitch clearly wasn't in the mood to debate things, and for once I figured I'd go easy on him and listen. Besides, he was right. There wasn't anything more for me to see. The burned area was completely taped off, and I didn't see anything to shed light on the killer's identity.

"Alright, I'll go. But don't think this means I'm giving up on the case."

Mitch made a sound that was somewhere between a snort and a laugh. "Don't worry. I'm not dumb enough to think that."

I made a face at him, but then turned to leave. No sense in dragging this pointless conversation out any further.

But when I turned on my heel, I turned a little too quickly and tripped over an uneven spot on the ground. To my utter embarrassment, I fell face first into the dirt, landing with a very loud, very unladylike thud. Mitch was by my side in an instant, chivalrously offering a hand to pull me back up.

"Are you alright?" he asked, suddenly seeming wide awake as concern filled his voice. I ignored the helping hand he offered and did my best to not appear embarrassed as I stood, although I was sure my cheeks were bright red.

"I'm fine," I insisted. "I'm just really tired, and it's making me klutzy."

Mitch couldn't help laughing at my expense. "Aren't you always klutzy, even when you're not tired?"

I glared at him as I sat up and started to brush the dirt off my pants, but then, I paused when a hint of blue sparkle caught my eye. I leaned over to peer at the spot in the dirt that was strangely shimmering blue in the early evening sunset.

"Hey, what's this?" I asked, reaching for the blue sparkle to see what it was. A split-second before I touched it, Mitch screeched at me.

"Stop! Whatever you're about to touch, *stop!*" Startled, I looked back at him in confusion. He was glaring at me.

"Come on, Izzy! For someone who claims to be such a good detective, you ought to know that if you see something that might be evidence, you shouldn't touch it without using gloves. You're going to put your fingerprints all over a piece of evidence at a crime scene!"

I felt my cheeks heating up even redder than they already had from my fall.

"I wasn't going to touch it," I insisted, even though I totally had been. "I was just trying to brush some dirt aside to get a better look."

Mitch gave me a look that said he didn't believe me, and I merely smiled sweetly at him in response. He knew as well as I did that I'd been about to touch the object, but I wasn't going to be too hard on myself about that. I was running on fumes at this point, and I wasn't thinking clearly. It had probably been a bad idea to come out here, but I was glad that I had in the end. If I had just found a piece of evidence, however small, then Mitch couldn't exactly be mad at me for being here, could he?

Mitch snapped a glove onto his hand, and used his gloved hand to pick up the blue sparkly object. He put it into a plastic bag labeled "Evidence," then held the bag up in front of his face to peer at the object. Without asking permission, I stepped closer so that I could see it, too.

It looked like a hairclip. The clip was long and black, except for the top portion which was decorated with an intricate array of sparkling blue stones.

"Wow," Mitch said. "Looks like perhaps our killer and arsonist is a woman."

I chewed my lower lip, and my mind's eye filled with mental images of both Sophia and Belinda. Had this clip belonged to one of them? Mitch's face grew dark, and I wondered if he was thinking the same thing. I didn't think he wanted to believe that Belinda or Sophia were murderers any more than I did, but so far they were the only ones with evidence against them, however meager that evidence might have been.

Mitch stared at the hairclip for a few more moments, then looked up at me. "I suppose you want me to thank you for finding this?"

"I wouldn't mind," I said a bit cheekily.

"Well, you're not going to get a thank you. I would have found this without you when I finished scouring the area, and you shouldn't be here. You should be home safe, or at your pie shop baking pies. Please, get out of here and go somewhere that I'm not going to be worrying about you."

I made a face at him. "It's not my fault you're a worrywart, and I don't believe you would have found that hairclip. It was a bit hidden in the dirt. But I'll go ahead and go. I don't think there's much more to see here, and I've had about all of your grumpiness that I can take."

I playfully stuck my tongue out at him to let him know that I was mostly joking, but he didn't laugh. In fact, he barely seemed to notice me. He was staring at the hairclip again, his brow furrowed in a worried look, and I decided it was time to go. I'd done my part here, and I'd gained at least a few new pieces of information. That was about all I could hope for.

Whistling to Sprinkles, I headed for my car, careful not to trip over my own two feet this time. As I climbed into my car, the remaining daylight was fading rapidly. The current heat wave made it feel like it was still summer, but the fact that the sky was getting darker earlier and earlier these days gave away the truth: soon enough the temperatures would drop as the carefree, ice-cream-and-sunblock-filled days of summer gave way to autumn. I shivered as I started driving away, and I wasn't sure if it was because the heat outside was dropping, or because my worries over this case were growing.

Mitch had been fairly tightlipped, as he always was, but even though he never talked much, I could tell from the look in his eyes that he had precious few clues. This case was frustrating him, and he knew as well as I did that the more time that passed, the harder it would be to dig up more clues.

I set my face in a determined line. That was fine. If things were hard for Mitch, that meant he would be all the more grateful when I solved this case.

And I was going to solve it. That killer didn't stand a chance with Izzy James on the trail.

I drove away from the lemon grove, not sure of how I was going to find more clues, but sure of one thing: I *was* going to find more clues.

CHAPTER TEN

On the way home, my overwhelming exhaustion finally caught up with me. Thankfully, I didn't fall asleep at the wheel. Nothing that serious. But I did take a wrong turn, and didn't realize it until I had gone about ten minutes in the wrong direction. Cursing under my breath, I looked over at Sprinkles to see why he hadn't alerted me to my mistake. Usually, he was pretty good about barking up a storm if I went the wrong way. That dog had the best sense of direction of any creature I'd ever known. But when I looked at Sprinkles, I saw that he had curled up into a little ball on the seat and fallen asleep.

"A lot of good you did me," I said. There was no reply from his slumbering form.

With a sigh, I turned around to head in the right direction. I knew one thing for sure: any more sleuthing would have to wait until tomorrow. Right now, I needed to head home and go to sleep. I'd somehow managed to make it through the day on fumes and caffeine, but I knew I wouldn't be able to do that two days in a row. My pillow was calling my name, and I was going to answer.

It didn't help that it was almost completely dark now. I turned on my brights, and squinted into the distance, wishing I had some toothpicks to keep my eyelids open.

Okay, I was kidding about the toothpicks, but only a little bit. I could not get home soon enough. A few moments later, another car appeared on the road, traveling in the opposite direction. With a grumble, I turned my brights down and tried not to look directly into its headlights, which seemed much brighter than they should be. I wasn't sure if it was because the driver actually had brights on, or because I was so tired, but either way I couldn't wait for the driver to pass me so I could once again turn on my own brights and see a little bit better.

But as the car approached, it looked like it was coming into my lane. With my heart beating fast, I was suddenly wide awake. I shook my head, and even gave myself a slap on the side of the face. Was I really that tired? Was I going crazy and thinking that this driver was on the wrong side of the road when they weren't?

Or was it possible that I myself was driving on the wrong side of the road in my exhaustion?

For the first time that evening, I thought that perhaps I should pull over and call Molly or Grams to come pick me up. It would be embarrassing to admit that I was literally too tired to drive myself home, but being embarrassed was better than getting into a wreck.

But as I squinted at the road in front of me, I could see that I was clearly on the right side of the road and in my lane. The double yellow line to my left and the solid white line to my right told me that I was exactly where I needed to be. It was the other car that was in the wrong lane.

"What the heck are you doing?" I shouted aloud, as though the other driver could somehow hear me. Of course they couldn't, and kept barreling toward me in my lane.

Unsure of what to do, I swerved into what should have been the other driver's lane, meaning I was driving on the wrong side of the road. But as soon as I did that, the driver swerved back. Cursing under my breath, I swerved back into my right lane. Perhaps when I had switched lanes the other driver had realized they were in the wrong lane and had corrected the mistake.

"Stupid driver," I muttered under my breath. "You probably had too much pinot down at Theo's winery or something."

But as I settled back into my correct lane, the other driver swerved back again.

"What the heck!" I swerved again as well, and started to slow down. I just wanted to get off the road until this person passed. The other driver must be drunk. There was no other explanation for it.

But even as I slowed, the driver continued driving forward in my lane. My heart was pounding now. If I didn't know better, I would think that this person was trying to force me to play a game of chicken. I started to slam my brakes. The other car was getting far too close for comfort, and there were no shoulders on the road out here. If I had to go off the road suddenly, I was going to be bouncing over uneven ground full of all sorts of brush, rocks and who knew what else.

Thankfully though, the other driver seemed to give up or realize what they were doing, and they went back into their lane. Letting out the breath I hadn't even realized I'd been holding, I muttered a string of curses.

Then, I screamed as the driver came back into my lane.

The next few seconds flashed by in a blur. It was too late for me to stop completely, and I could see now that there was another car coming behind the crazy driver. I couldn't switch lanes, and I was afraid to just go into the wrong lane again, anyway, because I had the feeling this lunatic would just follow me there. Was this person really risking a head-on collision?

With no time to think through my options, I made the best split-second decision that I could, and swerved off the road completely. As soon as my car hit the uneven terrain on the side of the road, I lost control.

I hadn't even been going that fast anymore, but you didn't have to be going that fast on this uneven ground to lose control. Sprinkles barked loudly, suddenly wide-awake, and I felt my heart lurch in my chest with fear. If something happened to Sprinkles, I would never get over the heartbreak of it.

"Sprinkles!" I yelped. He yelped back, and the next thing I knew I felt the car spinning wildly out of control. I ran into something—a tree? I wasn't sure—and I felt a sharp pain in my left arm.

The next thing I knew, everything went black.

CHAPTER ELEVEN

I blinked my eyes open, confused by the darkness around me, and by the sharp pain in my arm. My face felt strangely sticky, and I put my hand up to feel it. When I pulled my hand back, it was covered with some sort of semi-dried liquid substance. I sniffed at it, and that's when I realized it was blood.

In that moment, everything came rushing back, and I remembered the car that had been strangely playing chicken with me on the road. I groaned, and tried to look around. As my eyes adjusted to the darkness, I could see that my car appeared to have run into a small tree.

I was staring out at the world from a strange angle. I wasn't upside down, exactly, but I wasn't right side up either. I reached to try my seatbelt, and it stuck. The belt buckle had somehow been smashed, and the seatbelt wouldn't budge. Whimpering, I tried to wriggle out of the belt, but that only made the pain in my arm hurt more, and didn't get me a single inch closer to being free.

That's when I remembered Sprinkles.

My heart dropped as I twisted to look at the passenger seat. Sprinkles' side of the car was decidedly less smashed up than mine, but Sprinkles himself was nowhere to be seen. I twisted to try to look in the backseat, confused by how he just wasn't there. The front windshield was shattered, but still intact, so he couldn't have gone out that way. His door was closed, too.

I forced myself to scan his seat, terrified that I would see blood. As far as I could tell, there was no blood on his seat, although that didn't necessarily mean that he was okay.

But try as I might, I couldn't manage to get my body twisted to where I could see the backseat.

"Sprinkles?" I called softly. There was no answer. If he was in the backseat, he was unconscious. I tried not to think about other reasons he might not be answering if he was back there.

"Sprinkles!" I said in a much louder voice. Still no answer. I tried a few more times, calling louder each time. But there was no answer other than the occasional rustle of wind.

I looked around for my purse, hoping that I'd be able to grab my phone and call for help. But my purse was hopelessly out of reach. If I wanted to call for someone, I'd have to get out of the seatbelt. I tried again to wriggle out, and I tried again to unlatch the buckle. But neither attempt was successful. I closed my eyes, trying not to cry. Panicking wouldn't help me. I needed to keep a clear head.

I squeezed my eyes shut even tighter, and tried to think. But closing my eyes made me feel so sleepy. I was so tired, so very tired. It had been such a long day, and it had ended in such a crappy way.

Actually, it hadn't exactly ended yet. It couldn't end until I figured out how to get out of here and get to safety.

But the harder I tried to think of a solution, the fuzzier my brain felt. I found myself fighting to stay awake, until finally, I felt the blackness take me over again.

* * *

I had no idea how much time had passed when I came to once again. But this time, it was the sound of voices that brought me back to consciousness.

For a moment, I was perfectly still, trying to hear who the voices might belong to. Part of me was overjoyed that I might be saved, but before I called out, I stopped. What if one of the voices belonged to the crazy driver who had run me off the road?

And there was no doubt in my mind that someone had deliberately run me off the road. That person hadn't been drunk. They had known exactly what they were doing. It had been far too calculated and precise to be just the random swerving of someone who'd had too much wine. Was that person out here now, coming to make sure they'd finish the job of taking me out?

But the voices called out again, and this time I heard them clearly. "Izzy! Izzy! Izzzzzzyyyyyy!"

I could have cried when I realized that the voices belonged to Mitch and Theo. And then, in the next moment, I heard a bark. Then another bark, and another bark.

Tears of joy started streaming down my face. I would know that bark anywhere. It was Sprinkles! He must be alive and well if he was barking that robustly.

I tried to call out to Mitch and Theo, but when I opened my mouth to yell, I found that my throat was horribly dry. Only a pitiful, croaking sound came out. I tried to clear my throat and try again, but I still wasn't able to get much volume. It didn't matter, though. A few moments later, I heard the sound of footsteps coming toward my car. Then I heard Mitch's voice saying. "Holy crap, it's her car! It's completely smashed up!"

"Oh, no! No, no, no!" This time it was Theo speaking.

Both of the men sounded terrified, and I realized that they probably feared that I was dead inside the car. I tried once more to speak, to reassure them that I was alright.

Well, to reassure them that I wasn't dead, at least. I still wasn't exactly sure if I was alright. But at least I was still breathing, and as far as I could tell all of my limbs were still attached and movable.

A few seconds later, a bright flashlight shone into my eyes, and I instinctively put my hand up to block the light. When I did, I winced and howled in pain. I had forgotten that my arm was banged up so badly, and the sudden movement had sent shivers of pain all through me.

"Izzy! Are you okay? Are you alive?" Mitch sounded like he was on the verge of tears, which was strange since he always seemed like such a tough guy to me.

But when Theo spoke, he didn't sound much better. "Let me see! Does she need medical attention? I know CPR! We should call the paramedics and ambulance!"

Both of them were suddenly talking about one hundred miles a minute, and I wasn't able to get a word in edgewise. Weakly, I dropped my hand so they could see my face and see that I was at least alive.

A few seconds later, I suddenly heard a thump in the back of the car, and a few seconds after that, Sprinkles was right next to my face.

He sniffed me with concern, and gave me big, sloppy kisses on my cheek.

"Sprinkles! You're alright! I was so worried about you!"

I still couldn't see out toward the back of the car, but there must have been a door or window smashed open, because Sprinkles had obviously had no trouble getting in. That must have been how he'd gotten out as well.

Theo and Mitch finally stopped talking enough to take a good look at me, and realized that I was talking and breathing.

"How badly are you hurt, Izzy?" Mitch asked. "Can you move at all?"

"I think I'm mostly okay. My left arm hurts horribly, but other than that everything seems okay. There's some blood on my head, but it's dried so I don't think I have any critical open wounds. And I can wiggle all my arms and legs. The only thing is that I can't get out of my seatbelt. It seems to be stuck, and I'm totally pinned in."

"I see," Mitch said, already lowering his flashlight and reaching for the door handle. He tried to open the driver's side door, but it wouldn't budge more than a few inches.

"The tree's blocking it," he said. "Let me go around and try the other side."

As he went around to the other side, Theo's face appeared in the driver's side window.

"Are you sure you're alright? I already called an ambulance, just in case."

It took me a moment to be able to see his face, because I was still recovering from being blinded by Mitch's flashlight. But when my eyes did adjust and I could see Theo's expression, I was floored by how much concern filled his eyes.

I wasn't exactly sure how they had found me here, although I had a suspicion that Sprinkles had had something to do with it. But knowing that they'd both come for me, and were so worried about my well-being, brought tears to my eyes.

Theo was worried by the tears. "Are you sure you're okay? Just hang in there. We're going to get you out of there, and Mitch and I are both trained in emergency medical procedures."

"I'm okay. Just overwhelmed by everything. There was a—"

I was about to tell Theo about the car that had run me off the road, but before I could explain, Mitch was yelling at me.

"I'm going to pull the door! The car might shake, and I'm sorry if it hurts you a bit. But we've got to get you out of there."

In the next moment, Mitch pulled hard at the door, apparently expecting it to give him trouble. But thankfully, it flew open easily.

Within seconds, Mitch was beside me in the car, trying to undo the seatbelt. It wouldn't budge for him any easier than it would for me, and he cursed under his breath as he tried a few more times to jiggle the buckle open.

"Yeah, that's not happening," he said after a few tries, and he pulled out a pocketknife.

"Hold still," he warned.

I held perfectly still, trying not to whimper as I waited for him to cut me free. For the most part, I was alright physically. But emotionally, I was quite shaken. I was failing horribly at my efforts to keep calm, and if Mitch didn't get me loose soon, I thought I might completely break down. Not that anyone could have blamed me for it after everything I'd just been through, but still. I felt embarrassed at the idea of sobbing hysterically in front of Theo and Mitch, and I did my best to grit my teeth and remain calm.

Thankfully, it only took Mitch a few moments to cut through the seatbelt webbing. Once the seatbelt was gone, I was able to wriggle out of the awkward position the crash had left me in. I immediately started to do so, eager to climb through the passenger door and out to freedom.

Mitch, however, was concerned. "Wait a minute, Izzy. Are you sure you're alright? I don't know if you should be moving much until the paramedics get here. What if you have a spinal injury or something?"

I understood his concern, but there was no way I was staying in that car one minute longer. I knew I was fine, and I just wanted to get out of my wrecked vehicle and into the fresh air. I gave Mitch an annoyed look.

"You can either move out of the way and let me out, or I'll fight you until you let me out. And if I fight you, that's going to be a lot more stress on any potential injuries than just climbing out."

Mitch looked irritated, but he must have also seen the stubborn determination in my eyes. He grunted, cracked his knuckles, and then moved out of the way.

I stumbled out into the cool night air, taking several deep breaths as I tried to steady myself. I once again took a mental inventory of my body, trying to see which spots felt painful. My left arm was still throbbing, and I felt a general stiffness setting in all over my body—a stiffness I was sure would be even worse the next day—but otherwise I felt okay. All of my limbs seemed intact and unbroken, and there wasn't any damage to my neck or spine as far as I could tell.

Sprinkles ran in anxious circles around me, alternating between barking, licking my hand, and sitting close to me for a few moments with his very warm body pressed against me before taking off running in circles and barking again. I reached down to pet the top of his head, murmuring a few soothing words to him. But he was not easy to calm down at that moment, and I had no doubt that he knew how close he'd come to losing me.

It was also starting to hit me how close I'd come to losing him. I didn't know how he'd been lucky enough to escape that crash without being injured, especially since he hadn't had a seatbelt holding him in like I had. But Sprinkles had always seemed to be lucky, and thankfully that luck had held true during the crash. Not only had Sprinkles been saved, but he'd been able to save me. I shuddered to think how long I might have been out there alone if he hadn't been able to run and get help. And there was no doubt in my mind that he had been the one to go get Mitch and Theo. Even before they told me, it was obvious.

But the fact that it was obvious didn't stop Mitch from explaining.

"Theo and I were sitting at the winery after hours, enjoying a couple glasses of wine together," Mitch said. "Theo wanted me to try out this year's pinot vintage, and of course I was happy to do so—especially because he offered me a bottle of my favorite vintage in return for my opinion on this year's vintage. As we were sitting there in the tasting room, we heard a sudden scratching and barking at the tasting room's door. We went to see what all the commotion was, and it turned out it was Sprinkles."

Theo nodded and jumped into the conversation. "We knew as soon as we saw him that you were in trouble again."

"Hey!" I protested. "What do you mean *again*?"

Theo wiggled an eyebrow at me. "This isn't the first time Sprinkles has come running to my winery needing help in rescuing you from some predicament."

"Fair enough," I said sheepishly. I couldn't argue with that. There had been a few other occasions where Sprinkles had run to Theo to get help for me. I thought about making some smart aleck comment about how it was all part of the job for an amateur sleuth, but since Mitch was there I decided to keep my mouth shut. I was sure Mitch would not appreciate being reminded that I liked to sleuth around.

Thankfully, Theo dropped the subject of how often he had rescued me. Instead, he explained further about how the current rescue had happened.

"We put Sprinkles in Mitch's patrol car with the two of us, and let him guide us by barking. He led us to this spot, and at first we didn't see anything in the darkness. We thought he was a bit crazy for insisting we stop and get out of the car in the middle of nowhere. At least, that's what it seemed like he was saying by his barks. At that point we thought maybe we were misunderstanding him. But once we got out, he came running in this direction. A few moments later, we saw your car."

"I'm not sure I've ever been so scared in my life," Mitch said. "When I saw this car all smashed up and wrapped around this tree, I thought you were a goner for sure. I can't tell you how happy I am to see you alive and mostly okay. What in the world happened? You're not the type to drive crazy enough to lose control of the car like that."

In the distance, I heard the sound of sirens, and I knew that the ambulance Theo had called was on its way. I felt a bit embarrassed to have an ambulance coming out when I felt that my injuries were minor, but I knew it would make Theo and Mitch feel better if I let the paramedics check me out. I figured I owed them at least that much after they'd come to save me.

"I wasn't driving crazy. I was tired, yes. And I was admittedly starting to think that I should call Grams or Molly to come get me. But I just wanted to make it home, so I was driving as slowly and as cautiously as I could."

"Then what happened?" Theo interrupted.

"Someone ran me off the road." My voice started to tremble as I spoke the words. Saying it out loud brought back all of the terrified feelings I'd felt when I'd been staring at oncoming headlights in my lane. I paused, biting my lower lip and willing myself not to cry.

"What?!" Mitch exclaimed. "Are you sure? Was the other driver drunk?"

For a moment, I thought about passing it off as a crazy drunk. Mitch and Theo would be angry about that, but they would figure there was nothing they could do. Whoever the drunk person was would have been long gone by then. I wasn't sure exactly what time it was, but I was sure it had been a long time since my car crashed. It must have been at least two hours for Sprinkles to have had time to get to the winery on foot, and then for Mitch and Theo to drive back out. Whoever had run me off the road, drunk or not, was far away by now.

But I couldn't bring myself to lie to Mitch and Theo, even though I knew that telling the truth would make them both angry. I had a suspicion that whoever had run me off the road was somehow tied to Tom's murder, and it wouldn't be right for me to keep evidence like that from Mitch.

Besides, I was starting to get a little bit scared myself. How had that person known who I was and that I would be out on that road? Was I being stalked? And, if so, was it only a matter of time before this person struck again? I wouldn't feel safe until I knew that whoever this was had been caught, and telling Mitch would probably speed up the process of catching this villain.

"At first I thought maybe it was a drunk person," I said. "But when they swerved into my lane, I tried to swerve into the wrong lane to get out of their way. When I did that, they swerved back with complete control. No matter which lane I went in, they quickly went into that lane as well. They were clearly completely sober and able to make calculated lane shifts. They were just trying on purpose to scare me into running off the road."

"Apparently it worked," Theo said, his voice dark with anger. "I can't believe someone would do that! You could have been killed!"

I nodded soberly. "I think that was the point. I think that whoever did this wanted to take me out and make it look like an accident."

"But why? Who would do such a thing? You're one of the nicest people I know! I can't imagine anyone would want to hurt you." Theo's eyes were wide with shock as he spoke, but Mitch didn't look shocked by the news.

"I'll tell you who wanted to do that," Mitch said in a seething tone. "Someone who is afraid that Izzy is getting a little too close to discovering that they were the one who murdered Tom."

"Bingo," I said wearily.

I watched as this realization crossed Theo's face, and then he groaned. "Oh, Izzy. I wish you would leave this case alone. You're going to end up killed in your attempts to play detective."

Even though I knew that Theo had a point, I felt a twinge of anger at his words.

"This isn't a game to me," I said hotly. "I'm not playing. It matters to me that someone dangerous is on the loose in Sunshine Springs, and I'm just trying to help figure out who it is to help keep Sunshine Springs safe."

Of course, when I said that it only made Mitch angry. "It's the job of the police department to keep Sunshine Springs safe, and you shouldn't take this on by yourself! It's too dangerous, and we all would be heartbroken if something happened to you."

I forced myself to meet Mitch's eyes, although I didn't say anything in response. I knew he wanted me to agree to stop my sleuthing, but I wasn't going to do that. I also wasn't going to lie to him, which left us at a bit of a standstill. Before things could get too much more awkward, though, the sirens grew quite loud. I looked over to see that the ambulance was approaching the spot on the road near where my car had crashed.

As they screeched to a halt, the paramedics jumped out and started sprinting across the field toward us. Mitch and I both knew that there wasn't much time to continue our conversation right now, so Mitch merely gave me a pleading look and said, "We'll discuss this more later. But for now, will you at least promise me that for tonight you'll either go to Molly's house or your grandmother's house? I would feel better if you weren't alone."

I thought about insisting that I wasn't alone. After all, I would have Sprinkles with me even if I went home. But I figured that Grams might like having me over for the night anyway, especially after she heard what had happened. And if it would make Mitch feel better, then why not? Giving him a little bit of a concession now might make it easier to keep him off my back later.

And I knew there would be a later. There was no way Mitch was going to let this drop completely. Tomorrow, or the day after at the latest, he'd be chasing me down for a statement and admonishing me to stay out of things.

So, as the paramedics approached, I nodded my head in

agreement. "Okay. If it makes you feel better, I'll call Grams and stay with her tonight."

Mitch look relieved, and I felt a bit undone by the intensity of his gaze as he quickly murmured a thank-you.

The next half-hour went by in a blur. The paramedics asked me dozens of questions and ran all sorts of checks to make sure I was okay. In the end, they determined that there was nothing seriously wrong with me. My arm wasn't broken—just badly bruised—and the gashes I had were not deep enough for stitches. The paramedics got me cleaned up and cleared me to go home. By that time, Grams was driving up. Mitch had called her for me while the paramedics were checking me out, and of course she'd come as quickly as she could.

As I sank into the passenger seat of her car and Sprinkles jumped into the backseat, I closed my eyes and tried to stop the world from spinning. I had managed to mostly hold it together until now, but I wasn't sure I could do so much longer.

Thankfully, Grams knew me well enough to know that this probably wasn't the best time to pepper me with hundreds of questions. She reached over and patted my knee, then took off down the road without another word.

As we arrived at her house about twenty minutes later, I suddenly realized that it was just about time for me to be at the pie shop to start baking pies for the day. But when I tried to tell Grams that I needed to get to the café, she only laughed and shook her head at me.

"Oh, no you don't," she said. "You're going straight to bed, and I expect you to sleep for a long, long time. Then, when you wake up, I'm going to make you a big breakfast and you're going to relax for the entire day. No work for you tomorrow."

"But my pie shop!" I said. "I can't just close it for the day with no warning."

That wasn't strictly true. I had closed the pie shop with no warning a few times before. That was the benefit of owning my own business. If I absolutely had to, I could close the shop or change the hours on a whim. Of course, I didn't like to do that unless it was absolutely necessary. You didn't want customers to start thinking you were fickle.

But sometimes, life got in the way, and it was nice to have the option. I supposed that today was one of the times that life had gotten in the way, but I still wasn't excited about closing for the day.

I knew Grams wasn't going to let me argue about this, though. The determined look in her eyes was one I knew well: I got the same look in my eyes when I had my mind set on something.

But just because Grams was going to insist that I didn't work today, that didn't mean that she didn't understand my frustration over closing the pie shop. She gave me a gentle smile as she pointed me toward her guest bedroom.

"Don't you worry," she said. "I had a feeling you weren't going to want to close the shop, so I called Ruby. She agreed to go in and bake the pies and run the shop for you by herself today. She said she thinks that she has enough experience now to do so, and that if she does have any questions she'll just call. So you see, there's nothing to worry about. Your shop's taken care of, and now you need to take care of yourself."

"Really? You called Ruby? And she agreed to all that?" I had felt like Ruby and I had left on sour terms after the ice-cream shop. We hadn't exactly argued, but we'd definitely had a bit of a difference of opinion on how Mitch was running the investigation into Tom's murder. But now, it seemed that Ruby was rallying to my side to help me out when I desperately needed her.

Grams' smile widened. "Yes, she agreed to all that, and gladly. I would say you've got yourself a good employee there. I know it took you a while to find one, but I think Ruby was worth the wait."

I smiled weakly. "Yes, she definitely was."

I made my way to the guest bedroom, and barely kicked off my shoes before falling into the bed. I knew that within moments I would be asleep, and I wasn't sure I'd ever been so desperate for the chance to fall asleep. I knew that the next day was bound to bring plenty of its own worries, but for the moment I was alive and safe at Grams' house. Oddly enough, there weren't many people in the world who I felt would protect me as well as my old but feisty grandmother. She knew how to take care of her own.

Sprinkles also knew how to take care of his own. He followed me into the bedroom and flopped down beside the bed, curling himself up into a contented ball as he settled in. I knew he wouldn't be leaving my side anytime soon, and I was grateful for that.

I was grateful because I had a feeling that whoever had tried to kill me tonight was going to find out soon enough that I was still alive—and when they did, they were probably going to make a second attempt on my life. I shivered, and tried to push the thought out of my mind as I snuggled into the blankets.

But even as I drifted off to sleep, I couldn't quite shake the mental image of bright headlights barreling down the road toward me.

CHAPTER TWELVE

When I opened my eyes again, I could tell by the light streaming in the window that it was early afternoon. My head was pounding and my whole body ached, but as the events of the previous day came flooding back to my mind, all I could think was that I was so happy to be alive.

I sat up slowly, and found that Sprinkles was sitting up beside the bed, wide awake. He turned his head toward me as I stirred, then came rushing over to rest his head on the bed next to me. He covered my hand with wet, sloppy kisses.

"Hey, boy," I said with a smile. "You didn't want to leave my side, did you?"

He whined slightly in response, and I reached over to scratch behind his ears. As stiff as I was, it took a great amount of effort to get out of bed. But I knew that the longer I sat still, the worse the stiffness would be. I hobbled out to the main area of Grams' house with Sprinkles following inches behind me.

I found Grams in her kitchen, baking up a storm, and I almost had to laugh. Baking ran in the family. Just like me, Grams tended to bake like crazy when she was stressed. She made cakes and muffins while I made pies, but the general idea was the same. The more stressed she was, the more baked goods would appear in her kitchen.

If the amount of cakes, muffins, and cookies I currently saw were any indication, then Grams was feeling quite stressed. I felt a pang of guilt, knowing that it was because of me that she was feeling that way. But I knew that if I said anything about that, she would wave away my concerns. Grams was proud of my sleuthing efforts, and she wasn't the type of person to tell me to stop doing something because it might be dangerous. She always wanted me to stand up for myself and be brave. Without even asking, I knew that it was likely that her response to what I should do about last night's events would be something along the lines of "You should find out who tried to run you off the road and make sure they're caught so that they never run anyone else off the road ever again."

For now, Grams merely smiled at me when she saw me walking in.

"Sleep okay?" she asked.

I nodded. "I slept like a rock, and now I'm starving. I don't suppose you might be able to spare a few bites of one of these cakes for your hungry granddaughter?"

Grams grinned at me. "You can eat as much as you want. I made a few lemon cakes, and I've got freshly sliced strawberries that you can put on the cake. Breakfast of champions."

She winked at me and I grinned back at her. "Sounds amazing. Let me take a quick shower and change, and then I'll help you get rid of some of that lemon cake."

I still had a dresser of clothes at Grams' house, leftover from when I used to live in San Francisco and visited occasionally. When I moved to Sunshine Springs, I hadn't bothered to clear out the dresser even though I now lived just across town and never made overnight visits. But now, I was thankful that I hadn't cleared out the dresser. I felt worlds better after a quick shower and a fresh set of clothes.

After texting Ruby to make sure that everything at the Drunken Pie Café was going well—and being assured that everything was great and business was booming—I went back out to the kitchen. I saw through the window that Grams had headed out to her patio, where she was setting up a generous spread of food for me. In addition to the lemon cake and sliced strawberries, she had a pitcher of fresh sweet tea, a coffee carafe, yogurt, granola, and an assortment of cold cuts and cheese slices.

I went outside and shook my head in amazement. "This looks so good, but you really didn't have to do all this for me. I would have been fine with just a slice of lemon cake."

Grams came around the table and put her palms on my cheeks. "I know I didn't have to, but I wanted to. You need good food to get your strength back up. You've been through quite a bit. And what in my life could be more important than taking care of my granddaughter. You're the only family I have left, and I'm not going to lose you."

Her hair, currently an electric purple hue, sparkled in the sun. I felt tears starting to glisten in my eyes. Grams might be one of the most eccentric people I knew, but she was also one of the most caring. She was loyal to a fault, and I knew I was lucky to have her. I'd lost my own parents during college to a horrible car wreck, but Grams had always been there for me. Even when she'd been grieving the loss of her own son—my father—she'd been my rock. And now, here she was, being my rock again.

After a few beats of looking into my eyes, Grams gave me a little push toward one of the patio chairs.

"Sit. Eat," she ordered. "I'm just going to go freshen up for a moment and then I'll be back to join you. I must look like quite a mess after spending the entire morning in the kitchen."

I smiled at her. "I think you've never looked more beautiful, Grams."

She snorted, and then laughed. "What a good granddaughter you are to say so. But I beg to differ: I'm a mess. You eat, and I'll be back in a few minutes."

As she disappeared back into the house, I hungrily began stuffing food into my face. I started with the lemon cake, which was delicious as always. I had tried dozens of times to get Grams to give me the recipe for that cake, but she refused. She said it was a family secret that I would be given when she passed away. No matter how much I tried to cajole her into telling me now, she refused.

About ten minutes later, Grams came back out to the patio. She'd changed from her flour-covered apron into a brightly colored highlighter yellow dress, and she'd donned a flowery sun hat as well. She also wore a brightly colored necklace of hot pink and orange beads, and I couldn't help but smile when I looked at her. Grams' sense of fashion was a bit on the wild side, but I loved how she enjoyed dressing up even for a casual breakfast in the backyard with me. I looked down at my own t-shirt and jeans, then back up at Grams.

"I should have dressed up a bit more," I said.

But Grams waved away my comment. "Don't you worry. You

look perfect the way you are. I'm just glad to see you eating. Are you feeling better today?"

I nodded. "I'm still sore. In fact, I'm sorer than yesterday. But I feel like a new woman after sleeping and having a shower. And now, all this food is making me feel that much better."

Grams smiled, then removed her sun hat and set it aside. "I do love this hat," she said. "But the brim is so wide that it makes it hard to see you. And I have to say that it's so good to see you happy and smiling after everything you've been through."

Any reply I might have made stuck in my throat when I saw a sparkling blue hairclip in Grams' hair. My eyes widened as I squinted at it and realized that it looked exactly like the blue hairclip that I'd found at the lemon grove after the fire. I choked on the sip of coffee I'd just taken, and Grams looked up at me in alarm.

"Are you alright? Slow down, Izzy. We have all day and there's plenty of coffee. No need to gulp it down so rapidly."

I coughed, and took a few sips of water before replying. Even then, I chose my words carefully, because I wasn't sure how to approach the subject of the hairclip with Grams.

It was possible that Grams had worn a similar clip on the day of the murder, and had lost the clip at the lemon grove when she and I followed Sophia to the scene of Tom's unfortunate demise. In that case, there would be a perfectly benign explanation for the fact that a hairclip like that had been found at the crime scene.

But what if not? What if the hairclip I'd found the day of the fire was new? Then it might still be a good clue. Perhaps if Grams could tell me where the clip had come from, that would lead me to someone else who might be responsible for burning down the lemon grove. It might be a bit of a stretch, but it was worth asking about.

I cleared my throat, and smiled calmly at Grams. "Sorry. I guess I got a bit too excited with the coffee. I'll slow down a bit. By the way, that's a beautiful hairclip you have. I don't think I've seen it before. Where did you get it?"

Grams reached up and touched her hairclip with a smile. "Isn't it beautiful? You haven't seen it before, I'm sure. I only bought it yesterday. Sophia is selling them at her hair salon."

I nearly choked on my coffee again at this explanation. If Grams had only bought her clip yesterday then the hairclip at the scene must not have been a duplicate that she'd been wearing the day of Tom's murder.

The clip at the crime scene could have been from Sophia, though, since she was the one selling them. Sophia might have kept some of the clips for herself. But I frowned as I realized that if the clip had been Sophia's, then that didn't give me any new information. After all, everyone already knew that Sophia had also been at the scene of the murder. That's why she'd become a person of interest in the case.

The only way the hairclip from the lemon grove would be useful if it did indeed belong to Sophia was if I could somehow determine that the clip had not been lost at the grove on the day of the murder, but rather on the day of the fire.

"Hmmm," I said slowly. My mind was spinning and I wasn't sure what else to say. I didn't want to explain to Grams about the hairclip that I'd found at the scene of the crime, because I was worried I wouldn't be able to do so without sounding like I was accusing Sophia. I knew that Grams didn't believe that Sophia could possibly commit a crime like this, and deep down, I didn't either. Then again, I'd been wrong before about who could or couldn't possibly have committed murder. Grams had been wrong, too. Perhaps, we were wrong this time, and Sophia did have a darker side that no one had known about.

"What's the matter, Izzy?" Grams asked. "You look awfully troubled. Somehow, I don't think that worried face is just because you don't like my hairclip, although if you don't like it, that wouldn't be the first time you didn't agree with my fashion choices."

I couldn't help but chuckle at that. I never judged Grams for how she dressed, although I was compelled now and then to comment on how crazy her outfits were. It was always done in good humor, though. I loved how comfortable Grams was in her own skin, and I could only hope to be that way when I was her age.

"No, no. I love the hairclip. I just have a lot on my mind," I explained. "It's a bit of a unique hairclip. Do you know how long Sophia has been selling them, or if she's sold a lot of them?" Then, worried that Grams would be suspicious of my questions, I tried to act like I was just making small talk. "I just don't remember seeing them the last time I was in the salon, and they are quite beautiful."

For good measure, I shrugged, as though I really couldn't care one way or the other about the hairclips.

Grams touched the hairclip again. "Funny you should ask. Sophia actually mentioned to me that this was a new line of hairclips she's carrying for sale in the salon. In fact, yesterday was the first day she had them for sale. She said a woman came in and offered her a great deal on a bundle of them. Normally, Sophia doesn't do business with vendors who walk in to the salon without an appointment. But apparently, these clips were so beautiful and the deal was so good that she couldn't resist. At least, that's what she told me. She seemed a bit sheepish about the whole thing. It was almost as though she was embarrassed to have the clips there, and felt the need to justify them."

"Hmmm," I said, once again not sure how to respond.

It sounded like whoever had burned the lemon grove had bought a hairclip from Sophia's salon. It was always possible that someone else had had the hairclip before, and had been at the lemon grove the day Tom was murdered. But since Sophia hadn't been selling them then, the more likely explanation to me seemed to be that someone had bought a hairclip from Sophia's salon on the first day she started selling them and had then been wearing it out to the lemon grove when they set fire to the grove.

Had it been Sophia? She couldn't have sold the clip to that many people the first day, could she have? I hadn't even noticed the clips for sale myself when I had briefly been in the salon. Maybe Sophia herself was wearing one of her new clips while going out to burn the grove after closing up for the day.

But even as I mulled over all of this, I had to admit to myself that this was a big maybe. Any of the women in Sunshine Springs could have been in Sophia's shop and happened to buy a clip yesterday, which meant that any of them could be the one who had set fire to the grove. There was no way to know for sure who the owner of the clip from the grove had been.

I wondered, however, whether Sophia knew something more about this. Could she remember who the few people she'd sold hairclips to had been?

Or, more darkly, had it been her?

Even as I sat there, trying to act calm so that I didn't worry Grams, my mind was already racing with the possibilities. I decided that my next step would be to see what I could find out from Sophia, but I wasn't sure that I wanted to directly confront her. Instead, I started silently making plans to stalk her a bit. She'd been acting so strange, and I had a hunch that if I watched her coming and going a bit, I might see something that would be worth following up on. I had no idea what that something might be, but I had a gut feeling that there was more to what was going on with Sophia than met the eye.

I didn't want to worry Grams, so I changed the subject for the moment. I tried to discuss lighter topics while I finished eating, and when I was done with my food Grams tried to get me to go back to bed.

But I insisted I was fine. I was only a bit sore, and just the idea of trying to sleep right now made me feel a bit stir crazy. I told Grams that I wanted to check on the café, although I promised her I wouldn't actually try to work. I would just go see how Ruby was holding up. In an effort to support my business, Grams graciously agreed to let me borrow her car. My own car was unlikely to ever be driven again, but that was a worry for another day.

And yes, I would go by the café to see how things were—but only for a short bit. My real motivation was to go home and start planning how I would stake out Sophia's house.

I felt a bit guilty, because I felt that I was lying to Grams by not telling her this. I wasn't outright lying, of course. I would never do that. But I didn't feel comfortable telling her my plans. I didn't think she'd be happy with me for staking out Sophia, and besides that, I had a feeling that she would want me to at least hold off on my sleuthing efforts for another day or two until I was physically recovered. But I felt fine for the most part, and I was itching to keep working on this case.

I couldn't help but feeling that the longer it took to solve this murder case, the longer someone was out there wanting to murder me, too. Perhaps I was being a bit dramatic, but perhaps not.

One could never be too paranoid when there was a murderer on the loose.

CHAPTER THIRTEEN

Once I left Grams' house, I swung by the Drunken Pie Café to check on how things were going. After slow sales the last few times Ruby had been left in charge, I wasn't expecting much. I'd resigned myself to the idea that it was probably going to be a poor day of sales. But I told myself that poor sales were better than no sales, so I should still be grateful to Ruby for keeping the café open for me.

But to my surprise, the café was hopping when I arrived. The lines were just as long as ever, and Ruby was somehow managing it all by herself with a huge smile on her face. I saw her before she saw me, so I knew she wasn't just trying to look good because I was there. She seemed to genuinely enjoy working with the customers, and I felt a bit guilty for doubting her. Maybe she'd just had trouble the first few times she'd been working by herself and had now figured out how to handle the shop by herself. Or maybe it hadn't had anything to do with her, and she'd just happened to have a few slow days by sheer bad luck.

Whatever the case, today she looked like she was doing a magnificent job, and I breathed a sigh of relief. In the midst of all the frustrations and dangers that were currently filling my life, Ruby was a bright spot. I'd searched long and hard for a good employee, and I couldn't have been happier that I'd finally found one.

I didn't stay at the café long. I checked in with Ruby, who assured me that she had things under control and insisted that I go home to continue to rest. I figured she was right, and that I deserved the day off. Besides, I was eager to get to Sophia's house. I knew Sophia wouldn't be home yet, but if I got there before her, I figured I could find a good hiding spot to watch her when she came in.

And that's exactly what I did. Taking Sprinkles with me, I headed toward Sophia's house. I parked several blocks away, not wanting to take the chance that she would see Grams' car, realize I was there, and get suspicious. I walked with Sprinkles to Sophia's house, trying to look nonchalant in case I ran into someone. As far as anyone else could tell, I was just out for a stroll with my dog.

Still, the closer I got to Sophia's house, the more nervous I became. If any of her neighbors happened to see me, they might get suspicious. Word traveled fast in Sunshine Springs, and I had a feeling that people were already talking about the fact that I'd been run off the road last night. All it took was one of the paramedics mentioning something to another one of the paramedics while someone was eavesdropping. Soon, that eavesdropper would tell another person, and they would tell another person and so on until the whole town knew.

I shuddered. If Sophia was somehow involved in Tom's murder, would she be angered by the news that I was still alive? If she'd been the one trying to kill me, then she would know sooner than anyone that it hadn't worked. She always had the latest gossip coming through her hair salon.

I settled behind some bushes in Sophia's yard and felt a wave of guilt wash over me. Something about this didn't feel right. I had never known Sophia to be anything but friendly toward me. And while she clearly hadn't liked Tom that much, I couldn't imagine her actually killing someone. The pieces just didn't fit.

But if she didn't have something to do with all of this, then why did her name keep coming up as I followed the trail of clues? If I was honest with myself, I was hoping that I would actually find something that would clear Sophia's name. I didn't want to believe that she was truly capable of such awful acts.

I glanced at my watch, feeling more anxious by the moment. What would I find out today? When I looked at my watch, I realized I probably still had quite some time before Sophia would show up. It was another hour until her salon closed, and who knew how long closing duties would take her. I probably could have kept walking Sprinkles around for a while, but I didn't want to take any chances on not being around when Sophia showed up. I wanted to see how she acted when she came home, and whether she looked distraught or suspicious when she thought no one was watching.

Perhaps all of this was a long shot, but I wasn't sure where else to go from here. I was determined to see if this stakeout would yield any clues, so I stayed put. As I sat there, bored, my phone suddenly started ringing with an incoming call. I nearly jumped out of my skin, and realized that I would do well to put my phone on silent if I wanted to keep my stakeout a secret. The last thing I needed was for my phone to ring from the bushes right as Sophia was coming home from work.

I looked at my phone's screen to see who it was, but I wasn't intending to answer. I wasn't exactly in the best position to be chatting on the phone at the moment, so whoever it was could leave a message. But when I saw the name on the caller I.D., a rush of guilt washed over me.

Molly.

In my disoriented state last night, I had only called Grams. I hadn't texted Molly to let her know what had happened. I'd figured I would wait and let her know at a more reasonable hour. But when I'd woken up this morning—er, this afternoon—I'd been too focused on taking a shower, eating, and then figuring out the stakeout to think about Molly. Now, I realized that my best friend had probably found out about last night's mishap through the grapevine. She would be understandably upset about that. I knew that if I had found out something that serious about Molly through the gossip mill, I'd be irritated too.

Then again, could Molly really be that angry? She'd been acting so strangely lately, and every time I saw her our conversation was a cryptic mix of her telling me that she had some big thing to tell me combined with her telling me that she didn't approve of my sleuthing efforts. Could she really blame me for not contacting her about last night?

Okay, maybe she *could* blame me a little bit. But no matter what I should or should not have told Molly already, there was no way I was actually going to talk on the phone with her right now. If anyone knew I was hiding back here with Sprinkles, they'd think I'd gone crazy, or tell Sophia, or both.

Probably both. I wasn't going to chance it. I was going to sit here perfectly quiet until Sophia came home and I could spy on her for the evening.

It occurred to me then that I was acting slightly creepy. If Sophia wasn't the murderer, or wasn't connected to the murderer, then I was going to feel guilty for prying into her personal space. But I told myself that if Mitch had labeled her a person of interest, then it was reasonable for me to consider her a person of interest as well. And if I wanted to be a good detective, I had to consider all angles.

A few moments later, my phone vibrated with a message. Molly had opted to text me instead of leaving a voicemail. But even though the message was written instead of spoken, I could still tell from the "tone" that she was angry with me.

Is what I'm hearing true? Did you really get run off the road and crash your car last night? How is it that I'm just now hearing this? You should have told me! Are you alright? Are you at the café today? We still haven't had a chance to talk! I wish you would leave this case alone! Everyone has been telling you it's so dangerous, and I really think it's true. It's more dangerous than the other cases you've worked on. Please, Izzy, call me back as soon as you can. I'm so worried about you.

In a strange way, the message made me smile. It was written in a stream of consciousness sort of way, the exact way that Molly talked when she got excited about something. In that moment, even though I knew she and I were slightly on the outs, I couldn't help but miss her. I briefly considered inviting her to come sit with me outside of Sophia's house, but decided against it. She seemed pretty against investigating this case further, and she might just try to talk me out of being here. Or, worse, she might try to tell Mitch where I was and convince him to come get me. I couldn't take that chance.

I wasn't going to leave her completely hanging, though. I decided to send her back a vague but cheerful message.

Hey, sorry I haven't been in touch! Things were a bit chaotic after the crash. Somebody did run me off the road, but I'm fine now. My car is likely totaled, but luckily Grams let me borrow her car to get around today. I know you still want to talk, but I'm busy right now taking care of a few things. Perhaps we could meet tomorrow after the café closes?

I reread the message, then decided to also add a little smiley face emoticon, hoping it would take the edge off of Molly's irritation. I knew she was definitely going to be irritated when she saw that I wasn't interested in hanging out tonight.

As I expected, my text brought a flurry of texts from Molly about how she wanted to meet tonight, and asking how I could be too busy for my best friend, especially after what had happened the night before.

I winced as I read the texts. Molly was indeed my best friend, and was probably the best friend a girl could ask for. Even though things had been slightly strained between us over the last few days, I felt badly not telling her where I was. I considered breaking down and explaining things to her, but as my fingers hovered over my phone, I once again decided against it. I knew Molly would insist on coming out here if she knew where I was, and I just couldn't take the chance on my stakeout of Sophia being ruined.

I did make the small concession of admitting that I was doing some sleuthing. I knew Molly wouldn't be happy about that, but at least then I didn't feel like I was lying to her.

I'm really sorry that I can't meet with you tonight. After last night's crash, I had some clues I wanted to follow up on. I promise I'll tell you all about it when I meet with you tomorrow. That is, if you are open to meeting tomorrow?

There was a long, long pause. I started to think that Molly wasn't even going to answer me, but thirty minutes later, she finally texted back a single word.

Fine.

I sighed, knowing that I was going to have some work smoothing things over with her once I did finally meet with her. But I didn't see any other option at the moment than to stay vague.

My worried thoughts about Molly were cut short, however, when I saw that Sophia's car was approaching. My heart started pounding with excitement as I crouched even lower behind the bushes. I'd found the perfect hiding spot. I could peer out and have a good vantage point of the driveway, the front door, and the road, but I also could peek in a side window and see into Sophia's house.

Because Sophia's house was an open plan, I could see the living room, kitchen, and dining room from where I sat. I was hoping I'd be able to hear anything that might be happening inside as well, but I wasn't sure about that. I knew that the windows at my house were definitely thin enough to hear through, but I wasn't sure if the same could be said for Sophia's.

I would find out soon enough, because Sophia was currently pulling into her driveway. I held my breath, as though if I so much as breathed in and out she might hear me and know that I was there. As she stepped out of her car, however, I realized that I needn't have worried. She looked harried and distracted.

Even from my somewhat distant vantage point, I could tell that she had bags under her eyes. She clearly hadn't been sleeping much, but why? Was it because she'd been up late the night before? Was it possible she had been the one driving on the road in the wee hours of the morning? I shivered again despite the heat, and crouched down even lower. Sprinkles pressed his body against mine, as if to reassure me that he wouldn't let anything happen to me. I had to admit that I'd never been quite so happy to have him nearby.

I had a feeling that I might indeed find out something about Sophia tonight—and I also had a feeling that I wasn't going to like what I found.

CHAPTER FOURTEEN

As Sophia walked into her house, I peered into the window, careful to keep as much of my face as possible hidden.

Sophia rushed around her kitchen as though lost. She set her purse down and picked it up again several times. She put her keys in the refrigerator, then realized her mistake and pulled them out. She turned in nervous circles and I crouched even lower, worried that she might see me. I didn't know why she was so distracted, but I definitely didn't want to know how she might react if she realized that I was spying on her. She seemed a bit unstable, to put it mildly.

I watched her rush about like this for about ten minutes, and I was starting to think that I was wasting my time here. She didn't seem to be doing anything that would give me an indication of why she was so upset. I wondered how long I should sit before I considered this a useless exercise. But just as I was about to give up, Sophia's cell phone rang. The shrill ringer easily carried through the window, and I was delighted to find that not only could I hear the ringer through the window, but I could also hear her voice, just as I'd hoped.

"Hello?" Sophia said into her phone. Even though her voice was muffled slightly by the window, I could tell that her voice was shaking. Something was bothering her, and I was hoping that perhaps she would talk to this caller about whatever it was.

There was a pause as Sophia waited for the person on the other end of the line to speak, and I squirmed in my hiding spot, wishing that I had some way to know who the caller was and what they were saying.

It felt like forever before Sophia spoke again, but finally she did. I held my breath as I strained to hear what she was saying.

"Look, no one can hear about this though, okay? Please, tell me that if we do this deal and refinance everything, that things will be kept quiet. It's a horrible interest rate, and you know it. But I'm willing to pay it if it means that you'll promise not to blab about this deal to anyone else. You know how people in Sunshine Springs are. If they catch wind of this, everyone's going to know, and I can't let that happen."

I perked up even more, wondering what in the world Sophia was talking about. What was she refinancing? Her house? Her salon? And why didn't she want anyone to know?

There was another long pause. I squirmed impatiently, hoping that Sophia would say something else and give away more information on what she was talking about. As I watched her, her face grew more and more upset. Finally, she started to speak again.

"That's not good enough!" she said, her voice rising and her face growing red with anger. "I'm not giving you my business unless you promise me it will absolutely be kept confidential. Aren't there privacy laws about this sort of thing? You just can't tell everyone in town about my financial business!"

There was another short pause, and then Sophia was angrily speaking again.

"You know exactly why! This isn't just about my reputation as a responsible business owner in the community. Sure, that's important to me, but this is about so much more! Mitch has all but accused me of murder. If it gets out that Tom had me in such a tight spot and that I was foolish enough to gamble money on all these real estate deals, then I'll be found guilty for sure. Everyone will think I killed Tom to get out of the bad financial situation he'd pushed me into."

Sophia was once again silent as she waited for the caller to speak, but this time I was okay with that. It gave me a few moments to process what I'd just heard her say. It sounded like she'd been involved in real estate dealings that had gone bad, and that Tom had been the one behind those real estate deals.

This struck me as a bit odd. Sophia had always seemed so financially responsible, and her salon certainly did well financially. There didn't seem to be any reason that she would be in any sort of dire financial straits, but I supposed you never knew from the outside what people's finances were really like. Was it possible that Sophia had gotten tangled up in some sort of shady deal with Tom and had thought the only way out was to kill him?

I shook my head slowly. All of this still seemed like a stretch. No matter how bad off Sophia might be financially, I couldn't see her killing someone over money. But my thoughts were cut short once more as Sophia began speaking yet again.

"I know it was a gamble! And I know all too well that I lost that gamble. But I need to get back on my feet, and I'm willing to pay you all this extra interest to do so if you'll just keep quiet about why I asked for the loan. I don't understand why it's so hard for you to promise that. The last thing I need is everyone in Sunshine Springs talking about how Tom had me backed into a corner where my finances were concerned. Everybody already knows I didn't like him, and if they know the full reasons why and realize that I was about to lose my house and my shop to him, then I'm doomed. Everyone will think I had the motive to kill him."

I couldn't keep my jaw from hanging open as I listened. A sick feeling started to swell in my stomach, and I almost wished that I hadn't heard what Sophia had just said. I didn't want to believe bad things about her, but the more I heard, the more I couldn't deny that this sounded bad.

I still didn't know who Sophia was talking to, but I had a feeling it must be someone from the bank in Sunshine Springs. If so, Sophia was right to be worried that they might talk. Even though financial information should be kept private, I wouldn't put it past some of the bankers here to think it was okay to blab about supposedly private information.

Sophia was once again talking, and it sounded like she was wrapping up her conversation with the caller. She promised to get some paperwork faxed over within the next day, and then that was it. She ended the call, and afterwards stood for several minutes in her kitchen, wringing her hands. I couldn't believe how distraught she looked.

Suddenly, the chaos and disarray in her house made more sense. She must have been so stressed about things that she hadn't had time to properly clean and keep her house organized. As for her lack of groceries, I wasn't sure whether she truly hadn't had time to get them, or whether she actually couldn't afford them. I never would have believed that Sophia couldn't afford groceries. She'd always come across as a savvy businesswoman with a successful salon. But maybe if she'd lost most of her money on a bad real estate deal with Tom, she truly was too poor to buy food right now.

I felt a mixture of pity and angst as I watched her pacing. It didn't take a genius to see that Tom had put her in a really tough spot. But had Sophia made that tough spot worse by harming him? Or was his murder completely unrelated to Sophia's issues with him?

I needed more evidence to know for sure, but it didn't look like I was going to be getting any more clues from Sophia right now. As I watched, she suddenly grabbed her purse and made her way toward her front door. With her face looking even more worried than it had before, she headed to her car, muttering under her breath the whole time. Then she revved the engine and sped away, leaving me sitting alone with Sprinkles and feeling even more confused than before.

I didn't move right away, but rather continued to sit in my hiding spot as I considered what to do next. Even though I knew it probably wasn't the smartest idea, I decided to see whether I could get into Sophia's house and find out any more information. Mitch would kill me if he knew I was trespassing on a suspect's house, but what Mitch didn't know couldn't hurt him, right?

Since I'd watched Sophia leaving and locking the front door, I knew it was locked. But I tried it anyway just to be sure. Finding that it had indeed been securely locked, I made my way around to the back door, but that door was locked, too. I tried a few windows, and a side door in the backyard that must have led to the garage. Everything was locked, and my shoulders slumped down in defeat.

I didn't have it in me to actually break down Sophia's locked doors. If I'd been able to just walk into her house that would have been one thing, but I wasn't going to actually break in. Perhaps it wasn't a big difference either way, but it felt like one to me.

"Come on, Sprinkles," I said. I almost felt relieved that I didn't have the option of trespassing. It wasn't the right thing to do, and I knew it. But this case was driving me crazy, and I was more worried for my own life with every passing moment. Fear was causing me to consider doing things I wouldn't normally have done.

As I walked back to my car, I felt that fear growing with every step. I had to do something, and fast. But what? Should I confront Sophia and hope that she would crumble and tell me everything? But if she was the killer and I confronted her, she might hurt me to keep me quiet when she realized I knew more than she wanted me to.

But then, another idea took root in my head. What if I went to ask Belinda about Sophia? It was true that there was a possibility that Belinda had harmed Tom. She had been the one to set up the scavenger hunt, after all. Even though the clues had been changed, it was possible she herself had been the one to change them to try to throw people off her trail.

Was Belinda the one trying to kill me? I didn't know whether or not I believed that Belinda was more or less likely than Sophia to be the killer. But perhaps I could talk to Belinda and ask her what she knew about Sophia.

If I could get some information about Tom's real estate dealings with Sophia, perhaps I could help clear up this case a little more. And surely, if I sounded like I was accusing Sophia, Belinda wouldn't be too upset with me—even if she herself was the guilty party.

It was a bit of a risky plan, but I thought the risk would be manageable. And no matter how much Molly, Mitch, Theo, and Scott tried to warn me, I couldn't keep out of this case—especially now that I knew that things were personal.

Whoever had tried to kill me had made one big mistake: they'd failed. Now, I knew someone was after me, and I was going to make sure I found them before they found me again. I was the best amateur sleuth in Sunshine Springs, and I was determined to prove it.

CHAPTER FIFTEEN

I drove Grams' car over to Belinda's house, and had strange flashbacks as I pulled onto Belinda's street. In the last murder case I'd worked on, Belinda had been a suspect as well. She'd been proven completely innocent, so I shouldn't hold it against her. But I still had a strange, unsettling feeling as I made my way toward her house.

I felt an especially fresh pang of guilt when I realized that Molly had been helping me sleuth the last time I'd been here. Perhaps I should have called Molly to come with me this time, too. I didn't think that walking right up to Belinda would be as dangerous as staking out Sophia's house, and perhaps Molly would have agreed about that and come with me. No matter how much Molly told me to stay out of this case, I had a feeling that she wouldn't be able to help her curiosity if presented with the chance to talk to a suspect. Molly could tell me not to sleuth all she wanted, but at the end of the day she liked a good mystery as much as I did.

I was already at Belinda's, however, and I figured it was best to just head up to the door and see what I might be able to find. With Sprinkles trotting along beside me, I felt a little less afraid, and I raised my hand to ring the doorbell. But before I could press the ringer, I was stopped by the sound of loud sobbing. I froze with my hand in midair, unsure of what to do. Was that Belinda sobbing in there?

With a growing feeling of trepidation, I pressed my ear against the door, hoping that if it was Belinda sobbing, that she'd be too distracted by whatever was upsetting her to realize that I was at the door.

I had to strain hard to understand what was being said, but if I tried really hard, I could make out the words.

"I just don't know what I should do," Belinda said in a sobbing voice. "It's so unfair. I gave up my entire life for Tom! Frank and I had been married for so long, and had built a life together. But Tom promised me that he would make leaving worth my while. I was such a fool, but everything with him was so exciting and new, and it had been so long since I'd felt that sort of excitement. I couldn't believe it when Tom started threatening to leave me!"

At that point, Belinda dissolved into more hysterical sobs. If she *was* still trying to talk, I couldn't understand what she was saying.

I strained even harder to understand, but it was useless. Then, however, to my great shock, I heard a voice that I knew all too well—Ruby's.

"You're worrying too much," Ruby said soothingly. "Everything's going to be fine, I promise."

Belinda kept on sobbing, and I stood there with wide eyes. Perhaps I shouldn't have been surprised to hear Ruby. I knew that she and Belinda were good friends, so if Belinda was in need of comforting, of course Ruby would be there. But I didn't want to talk to Belinda with Ruby around. I hadn't forgotten how Ruby had disapproved of Mitch's investigation of Tom's murder, and I had a feeling that Ruby would not approve of the way I was going about things with my own investigation. I didn't want her to know that I was involving myself so much in the case, and so I started to slink away from the door even more. I was surer than ever that I didn't want to get caught here.

And yet, my curiosity took over. It sounded like Belinda was baring her soul to Ruby about her relationship with Tom, and it sounded like that relationship hadn't been as wonderful as Belinda had led everyone to believe. This made me curious once again as to whether Belinda had been the killer. Had she been overwhelmed with anger or frustration because she'd given up everything for Tom and things weren't working out as well as she'd hoped?

I couldn't leave now. I had to know what else Belinda might have to say about this. Instead of heading back to Grams' car and driving away, I started heading toward a side window of Belinda's house. I was going to have a ridiculously hard time explaining what was going on if anyone caught me out here, but I didn't care. I'd just do my best to be quiet and keep anyone from seeing me. My only real concern at the moment was learning exactly what had been the issue between Tom and Belinda.

Sprinkles crept behind me as I made my way to a window and peered inside. From my new vantage point, I could see that Belinda and Ruby were sharing a bottle of wine, although it looked like Belinda had had quite a bit more to drink than Ruby. Ruby appeared to be sober for the most part, but even from this distance I could see that Belinda's eyes were glazed over and red. Belinda's hair was also a mess, and her clothes looked quite rumpled and wrinkled.

In contrast, Ruby looked bright-eyed and alert. She must have come directly from the café, because it wasn't that late and she wouldn't have had much time to go home and change. But still, she looked fresh and put together. Her hair was pulled back into a neat bun, and her clothes looked crisp and ironed. I couldn't remember what she'd been wearing earlier at the café, because she'd been wearing an apron over it and I hadn't looked that closely. But if this was how Ruby had dressed for work, then I was pleased with her effort to look presentable for customers.

Right now, all of her effort was focused on calming Belinda, who was more and more beside herself with every passing moment.

Despite her hysterics, though, Belinda did finally manage to begin speaking again.

"It's not okay," Belinda exclaimed. "Don't you understand? Apparently, Tom was talking to some people about how he was tired of me. If word gets around to Mitch that Tom and I were having troubles, he's going to see it as a motive to kill Tom! He's going to think that I panicked because Tom was threatening to leave me, and murdered him so that he couldn't leave."

I watched as Ruby shook her head reassuringly. "Don't be ridiculous, Belinda. Nobody is going to think you killed Tom just because you two were in a bit of a rough spot. Clearly, you were trying to work on it. For crying out loud, you put together an elaborate scavenger hunt for him."

Belinda sniffed. "Yes, but what if somebody thinks that the scavenger hunt was put together as a ruse to make people think that things were okay between us? I'm already coming under fire for the changed clues, as though *I* was the one who did that! Can you believe that? Here I am, dealing with the loss of the love of my life, and Mitch has the audacity to imply that I changed the clues. He thinks I wanted to make it look like somebody else interfered with the scavenger hunt to kill Tom, but that it was really me changing everything up all along."

Belinda started sobbing again, and Ruby once again patted her hand reassuringly, not at all surprised to hear Belinda talking about the changed clues. Belinda must have filled her in about that since I last talked to Ruby. Now, Ruby shrugged as she spoke to Belinda. "Don't worry so much about it. I know it's annoying, but Mitch has to do his job."

My eyes widened at these words. Ruby's attitude tonight was quite changed from her angry tirade against Mitch at the ice-cream shop just yesterday. I frowned, and wondered why she was acting so differently. It seemed odd that she'd had such a sudden change of heart regarding Mitch, although perhaps she hadn't so much had a change of heart as much as she just wanted to stay calm for Belinda's sake. Belinda looked like she could use as much calmness as possible right now.

Ruby's calmness didn't seem to be having much of an effect on Belinda. She seemed as upset as ever, if not more, after Ruby spoke.

"Mitch isn't just trying to do his due diligence!" Belinda sobbed. "He's out to get me. He's been out to get me for a long time, just like everyone else in this town. No one can accept the fact that I left Frank. They all think Frank's so perfect and I'm so awful. But my relationship with Frank wasn't anyone's business but mine and Frank's. It's completely ridiculous that people judge me and think that I'm the sort of awful person who might have actually killed someone!"

"It is ridiculous," Ruby agreed. "But don't worry. I heard that Mitch has been on Sophia's trail as well. I know that when he investigates her, he'll find plenty of evidence to show it was her and not you."

Instead of looking reassured, Belinda actually looked rather stricken by Ruby's words. "Do you really think it's possible that Sophia would do such a thing? I know you don't know her as well as most who have lived in Sunshine Springs their whole lives, but surely you can see that she's a decent enough lady. I know that Tom wasn't her favorite person, but I just can't imagine that she would actually kill someone."

Ruby's face darkened considerably. "Well, you better start imagining it, because it's the only explanation that makes sense. She didn't like him, and she was mad that he took you away from Frank. You know she was quite vocal about that."

"She was," Belinda said slowly. "But—"

"But what?" Ruby interrupted, her voice suddenly dripping with venom. "I'm telling you, Belinda: you and everyone else in this town seem to be blinded to Sophia's true nature. Maybe it's an advantage that I'm an outsider. I can see things you guys can't. I can see that Sophia isn't as nice as everyone seems to think she is. And I'll tell you another thing: I don't know what it was, but there was something more making Sophia angry at Tom than just the fact that he took you away from Frank. I can't quite put my finger on it, but there was something else there. And I have no doubt that when Mitch actually starts investigating her, he's going to find out what that something was. Everyone's going to be shocked, but I won't be. I can see clearly that Sophia isn't as innocent as everyone in this town thinks she is."

Belinda sniffed, and seemed to sober up a bit at that thought. "You really think so?"

Ruby nodded. "I'm sure of it. Don't you worry. Mitch will find out the truth, and Sophia will be found guilty. Everything is going to be alright, I promise."

Belinda took a slow sip of her wine, and seemed to calm down even more.

Ruby reached over and squeezed Belinda's upper arm. "Listen, do you think you'll be alright now? I hate to leave you, but I really need to get going. I have a few things I need to take care of, and I've been quite busy since Izzy wasn't able to make it to the pie shop today."

At the sound of my name, I felt my heart pounding. I irrationally felt like the fact that they were talking about me made it more likely that they would realize that I was outside eavesdropping on them. But neither one of them looked in my direction, of course. Instead, Belinda sadly shook her head.

"Can you believe that? Who in the world would want to hurt Izzy? Sure, she can be a bit nosy when she's trying to act like a detective. I know that all too well," Belinda paused and laughed, apparently amused by the memory of the last murder case I'd worked on, when I'd thought Belinda might have also been guilty.

But Belinda's laugh faded away as her face took on an expression of disbelief. "But still. Nosy or not, she's a nice girl. Who would want to hurt her?"

Ruby's eyes darkened. "Someone who is worried about Izzy solving the murder, that's who. But enough talk about the murder for now. Once you finish this wine, order yourself a pizza, watch a movie, and relax. You need to do something besides sit here and think about the murder case over and over again."

I saw Belinda sigh, then nod her head. "You're right. I do need to settle down, and pizza and a movie are probably the perfect way to do that. Thanks for coming by." She stood to bid Ruby goodbye. "I don't know what I'd do without your friendship."

Ruby smiled warmly at her and gave her a hug. As she hugged Belinda, she turned her face toward the window I was peeping in, and I felt my heart stop as I quickly ducked down. I thought for sure that she had seen me and was going to say something to Belinda, and I debated whether trying to make a run for it would make the situation worse or better. But I must have been wrong, and Ruby must not have spotted me. She didn't say anything to Belinda. Instead, Ruby gave Belinda a few more reassurances that everything was going to be okay, and then made her way out the front door.

I sat there for several minutes, holding my breath and not believing that I really hadn't been caught. Once I finally calmed down, I stood and peeked in the window again. Belinda had turned on Netflix, and was scrolling through available movies to watch. For a moment, I considered still knocking on the door and talking to her, as I'd originally planned. But after considering this, I decided it was better to wait. For one thing, Belinda had been awfully upset, and I wasn't sure that now was the best time to talk to her. If I started peppering her with questions about Sophia, she might get upset all over again. Not only that, but I wanted to think over everything now that I knew that Belinda and Tom had been having trouble. I felt it would have needed to have been quite a bit of trouble for Belinda to murder Tom over it. But I also felt that it would have needed to be a truly awful real estate deal for Sophia to murder Tom. Neither of these options seemed any likelier than the other, and I was starting to think that it was time to loop someone else in on this investigation for a second opinion.

Mitch might have been the obvious choice, but I wasn't going to talk to him. Not yet. I wasn't in the mood for another lecture on staying out of things.

Instead, I'd talk to Molly. She would appreciate being looped back into things, and although she seemed especially worried about this case, I knew that she wouldn't be able to resist a good mystery. If I explained all of the clues and information I had, she wouldn't be able to stop herself from giving me an opinion.

When I reached Grams' car, I texted Molly. My fingers trembled with excitement as I did.

Hey, are you still available to meet tonight? I have some information about the murder case, and I thought you might be interested in hearing about it.

I hit send and waited anxiously. I thought for sure that Molly would meet with me, since she had wanted to so badly before I staked out Sophia's house. But when Molly's reply came in, she wasn't as eager to meet as I'd thought.

Sorry, I already made other plans for tonight. I can still meet with you tomorrow, though. And please, can you lay off on the sleuthing? I'm worried about you! Someone's out there trying to kill you, and it would be best if you lie low.

I reread the message, not quite believing that Molly was turning me down. I shouldn't have been surprised. After all, I had turned her down a bit rudely earlier today, and it was getting late at this point. Of course she had already made other plans. But with whom? Scott? The two of them seemed to be hanging out without me quite a bit lately, and while this was partially my fault since I was always too busy to hang out, it still irritated me. Now, I felt much more irritated than I had the right to be, since I was the one who had originally declined Molly's invitation. Still, I felt left out, like all the cool kids were hanging out without me.

Feeling glum, I dropped my phone in the car's center console and decided to head home. Grams had told me that she didn't need her car back until tomorrow afternoon, and by then I hoped to be able to get a rental car. For now, I just wanted to get home.

Perhaps I would bake some pie to help calm myself down. I had some new recipes that I wanted to try, and although I probably shouldn't be taste-testing any more baked goods today after everything I'd eaten at Grams' house, the thought of being in my own kitchen at home and creating new pie masterpieces made me feel instantly calmer.

I furrowed my brow. Molly could hang out with Scott or whomever she wanted. It was fine. I wasn't jealous.

Okay, maybe I was a little bit jealous. But I had to admit that Molly was right about one thing: it was probably wise for me to stay home and keep a low profile tonight. Telling myself that I was doing the best thing given the situation, I drove home with plans to settle in for a night of baking.

I just hoped that, for once, my plans wouldn't be unexpectedly changed by something related to Tom's murder case.

CHAPTER SIXTEEN

An hour later, I had completely immersed myself in a spiked Christmas pie recipe. Christmas might have been a few months away, but I already felt behind on finalizing my holiday menu. There were a few recipes I'd been meaning to try for weeks. Usually, I was quite good at coming up with creative holiday menus, but I was feeling a bit nervous this year. The holiday menus I'd made in previous years had always been for dinner parties at home, so I'd never tried out my holiday pies on a larger scale at a bakery. This holiday season would be the first true test of my creative baking abilities, and even though I'd had quite a bit of success at the café so far, I couldn't help but worry that I might not pass this test.

I'd already expressed these concerns to both Molly and Grams, and both of them had assured me that I could do no wrong when it came to pies. And yet, I still worried.

The best thing for me to do when I was worried about a recipe was to bake it over and over. If I made the same recipe several times and it tasted good every time, then I figured I had a winner. This was my first attempt at this new spiked Christmas pie recipe, so I had a ways to go before I would consider it fully vetted for use at the Drunken Pie Café. But if the way it smelled was any indication, this one was going to be a winner. I smiled as I went to peek into the oven and saw that the pie's crust was starting to turn golden.

Feeling much better, I decided to reward myself with a bottle of wine and some good music. I had been so focused on getting the pie done that I hadn't wanted to interrupt my concentration with any wine or music. But now that the first pie was safely in the oven, I let loose a little.

I turned on my favorite jazz and popped open a bottle of my favorite pinot from Theo's winery. I poured myself a glass and took a long, luxurious sip, closing my eyes briefly to savor it. Theo might have his moments of arrogance, but no one could deny that his vineyard made a good wine. After the day I'd had, it felt good to relax with a glass of red, and I closed my eyes tighter as I took another sip.

My relaxation was abruptly cut short, however, by the shrill ringing of my cell phone. I had turned the ringer back on just in case Molly called and had time to meet, after all. I figured the caller must be either her or Grams, and I snatched my phone up without bothering to look at the caller I.D.

"Hello?" I said, as I crossed the room to lower the volume on my jazz music, which I hadn't realized was a bit loud until the call had come in. But it wasn't Grams' or Molly's voice that sounded in my ear. Instead, it was a familiar male voice.

"Izzy! Where are you!? Are you alright? Please tell me you're alright!"

"Mitch?" I looked down at the caller I.D. It was definitely Mitch, but he sounded panicked, which was not his normal mode of operation. In fact, he sounded even more panicked now than he'd sounded last night outside of my totaled vehicle. I put the phone back up to my ear, and must have sounded confused as I spoke. "I'm just at home, and I'm fine. Why? What's wrong?"

"Are you by yourself?"

"Yes. Well, I have Sprinkles with me, but there's no other person here. Why?"

"Listen to me," Mitch said, without giving me any further explanation. "I want you to make sure all your doors and windows are locked. Stay by the phone, and keep Sprinkles right next to you. I'm coming to get you."

I felt my heart starting to pound. This did not sound good. "Mitch, tell me what's going on."

"Just sit tight, and I'll explain everything when I get there."

Even through my fear, and even though I knew better than to question Mitch when he sounded like this, I couldn't help arguing with his directives.

"Tell me what's going on, or I'm not going to just sit here locked in like a crazy person."

"Izzy, please! For the love of all that's holy, can you just listen for once?"

"Nope. Tell me what's going on, or I'm not listening."

There was a long pause on the other end of the line, followed by a long sigh. Finally, Mitch spoke again, sounding irritated but resigned. "Someone called in a break-in at your pie shop. I obviously sent officers there right away, but I wanted to try to reach you to make sure you're okay. Given the events of last night, I was worried that you might have been at the pie shop late, baking or something, and that someone had gone there to try to hurt you. If that's what the break-in was all about, then my guess is that this criminal's next stop will be your house. Just keep your doors locked and don't let anyone in. I'll be there in less than ten minutes."

My heart felt like it was going to pound out of my chest, and a mixture of fear and anger washed over me. Of course, I was now terrified that someone was coming for me at my house. But I was also enraged that someone would have broken into my café. If it was Tom's murderer coming back to try to take me out again, they had been pretty stupid to go to the pie shop. It was so late at night that I had no reason to be there. But even though I should have been feeling thankful that I was safe, all I felt was violated.

"How did they break in? Did they break the door? Did they take anything? How could someone do this?"

"I don't know, Izzy. I don't have a lot of details yet. Like I said, I sent my officers over, but I haven't heard a report back from them yet. My biggest concern was finding out where you were."

"This is outrageous!" My anger was taking over my fear more and more with every second. "How could someone do this to my pie shop?"

Mitch's voice sounded gravelly as he spoke again. "I promise you that we'll find out who did this and make them answer for it. But for the moment I just want to get you safe. I'm almost to your place now. Have you locked the doors yet like I asked?"

But I was not interested in locking the doors anymore. All I wanted was to get to my pie shop and see what had been damaged.

"I'm not staying here," I said, already running toward the door and grabbing my purse on the way. Sprinkles bounded after me, letting out an excited bark or two.

"Izzy!" Mitch's voice came roaring through the phone. "This isn't a joke! There's someone out there trying to kill you! Please, stay put!"

"I'm not waiting around in fear for someone to come find me. And if they *are* most likely to come here next like you said, then why would I stay here like a sitting duck waiting for them to come get me? No way! I'm going to the pie shop. I want to see what they did. If you want to be near me to keep me safe, that's fine. But you'll have to come to the pie shop to do so."

Before Mitch could answer, I ended the call. I had to admit that my heart was racing as I exited my front door and made a beeline for my car. I half-expected someone to jump out and tackle me to the ground, shoving a knife or a gun in my face. But I made it to Grams' car without seeing or hearing anyone. I turned the key and the engine came alive with a roar that sounded abnormally loud thanks to my heightened state of adrenaline. I took a few deep breaths to try to calm down, then started backing out of the driveway as fast as I could.

"Here we go, Sprinkles," I said. "Let's see if this fool left any clues behind in the pie shop. This person has definitely gone too far if they think they can just break in and damage my café! They're about to see what Izzy James is made of!"

I slammed my fist angrily on the dashboard, and Sprinkles barked excitedly.

As I drove, I tried my best to stay brave, and not to think about the fact that there was a killer on the loose. I'm not sure I would have ever admitted it to Mitch, but I was glad that he was determined to stay close and keep me safe tonight.

I had a feeling I was going to need it.

CHAPTER SEVENTEEN

When I arrived at my café, two police officers were already there. Mitch, however, was nowhere to be seen. I stepped inside, glass crunching beneath my feet as I walked. The officers looked up, and I could tell from the surprised expressions on their faces that they had not expected me to be there.

"Izzy!" one of them said. "Mitch was looking for you."

I nodded. "I know. I talked to him and told him I was coming here."

I conveniently didn't mention the fact that Mitch had ordered me to stay home and lock up, and I had ignored him. It wasn't necessary for these officers to know that detail.

"We've done our best to comb through the scene for clues," the other officer said. "We've swiped for fingerprints as well, but there doesn't seem to be anything here to indicate who did this. I'm really sorry. It looks like they made quite a mess of things. I'm not even sure what they were after, because it doesn't look like they took anything from the cash drawers. Maybe you can take a look around and see if anything valuable is missing."

I nodded, and started to look around. Broken glass littered the floor everywhere, and all of the café's tables and chairs had been overturned. Several of my recipe books that I kept on the shelf behind the front counter had been thrown down onto the floor, but none of them were missing.

I looked carefully in the back room as well, but nothing had been stolen. Thankfully, the burglar had even left my office computer alone. It would have been a giant headache if they'd decided to steal that thing or smash it in.

I walked back out to the front of the restaurant to let the officers know that I hadn't found anything missing, but the words stuck in my throat when I caught a glint of sparkling blue at the very edge of the pastry case. Frowning, I walked over to investigate. My stomach did an uneasy flip-flop when I saw that it was exactly what I'd suspected. Perched on that pastry case's corner, in a fairly inconspicuous spot, sat a sparkling blue hairclip. It looked exactly like the hairclip that I'd found the day the lemon grove burned, and exactly like the hairclip Grams had been wearing earlier today—the hairclips that Sophia was supposedly selling at her shop.

A chill ran down my spine, and I bent over to look closer. This time, I remembered not to touch it so that the police could take it into evidence and fingerprint it, but I was confused as to how it had even ended up perched there. If it had fallen off of the intruder's hair, that would have been an odd place for it to land without clattering to the floor. Perhaps Ruby had bought the hairclip from Sophia and had been wearing it while she worked, then had taken it off for some reason and set it down. I'd have to remember to ask her about it, but in the meantime, I would have the police investigate and fingerprint this clip just in case.

I looked up to call one of the officers over, but before I could speak, I saw Mitch sprinting into the café with a wild look in his eyes. He frantically scanned the room, and when his eyes landed on me, relief flooded his face.

"Izzy!" he choked out, then ran across the room and pulled me into a giant bear hug.

In that moment, I suddenly felt horribly guilty. I had been so caught up in my own determination to figure out this murder case that I had not truly considered Mitch's feelings, or the feelings of anyone else in this town who cared about me. I'd put my own selfish excitement over the thrill of the chase above Mitch's worries and Molly's worries and Theo's worries. Scott was probably worried, too, although I hadn't talked to him much because I'd been so busy. I felt a pang of remorse, and remembered Grams telling me once before that if you can't make time for the friends you have, then you don't really deserve those friends.

I was starting to feel like perhaps I didn't deserve the friends that I did have.

"I'm really sorry," I said, feeling suddenly awkward. "I didn't mean to make you worry."

Mitch held me tighter, as though worried that if he let me go I'd run out of the pie shop and straight into the murderer, whoever they might be.

"Whatever you did or didn't mean to do, you scared the heck out of me," Mitch said. "I was terrified that I was going to get here and find that you hadn't even made it here because whoever this person is had found you and hurt you along the way."

"Nope," I said, trying to sound chipper. It didn't help that my voice was muffled by Mitch's chest. "I'm perfectly alright. Just ticked off that my pie shop is such a mess."

Mitch finally released me from his bear hug and pulled back to look into my eyes.

"Everything in here can be replaced," he said. "But if anything happened to you, we could never replace you."

I felt my cheeks heating up with embarrassment. It was starting to hit me just how childish I had acted. I couldn't change that now, though, so I gave Mitch a bright smile and said, "Well, on the plus side, I may have found another piece of evidence for you."

The look Mitch gave me told me that he could not have cared less about evidence in that moment. He grunted, cracked his knuckles, and gave me a weary look, as though he was too exhausted with me to even bother asking out loud what that evidence might be.

I turned and pointed to the hairclip, which still sat exactly where I'd found it. "Look, it's another hairclip, just like the one I found at the lemon grove. Don't worry. I haven't touched this one, so your officers can hopefully get some good DNA or fingerprint evidence off of it."

Mitch looked slightly more interested. "If these clips are from the criminal, you'd think they'd find a clip that would stay put better so they didn't keep losing them at the crime scene."

I chewed my lower lip. "Yeah. About that... I'm not sure that the clip is from the criminal. It's possible, I suppose. But this might just have been Ruby's clip. This morning, I saw that Grams has one of these clips, too. She told me that Sophia is selling them in her salon, so it's quite possible that all of the women in Sunshine Springs have these clips. I don't suppose finding a clip narrows down our suspect choices unless the clips from the crime scenes happen to contain some sort of fingerprint or DNA evidence."

Mitch nodded. "Yeah, my guess is that this clip probably belongs to Ruby. The other clip we found had some fingerprints on it, but they don't match any fingerprints in any of our databases. Sophia and Belinda both agreed to give me samples of their fingerprints as well, and the fingerprints from the hairclip at the crime scene don't match those prints. I have no idea who that clip belongs to."

Mitch motioned one of his officers over. "Hey, Smith. It's possible this hairclip might be evidence. Can you get a baggie for it?"

Officer Smith nodded and went to get an evidence bag. Mitch turned back to me, and cracked his knuckles once again. Usually, that sound annoyed me. But right now, I knew he was cracking his knuckles because he was worried about me. I could hardly fault him for caring, could I?

He frowned down at me. "Now that you've seen the pie shop, can I convince you to go somewhere safe for the night? I'd rather you didn't go home alone. Perhaps you could stay at your grandmother's house again, or maybe with Molly?"

I winced a bit at the mention of Molly. I wasn't sure that I deserved to stay at her place tonight, but that wasn't something I needed to trouble Mitch about. And I figured it couldn't hurt things to stay with Grams again—although I hated to worry her, and I knew she was going to be terribly worried when she heard that the pie shop had been broken into.

As I thought about this, Sprinkles suddenly barked. He was sitting by the front door in a spot clear of glass. Unfortunately, this wasn't the first time I'd had broken glass all over my café's floor, and he knew well enough not to walk across the broken glass. I looked up to see why he was barking, and a split second later I heard none other than Molly choking out my name.

"Izzy!" She ran across the café toward me, glass crunching beneath her shoes. Behind her, I was startled to see Theo and Scott as well. They all ran toward me, and when the three of them reached me they all enveloped me in a hug at the same time. I squirmed, feeling slightly embarrassed at all the attention I was getting.

"Guys, what are you doing here? What's this all about?"

"Scott and I were having ice cream at the ice-cream parlor out on the patio," Molly answered. "There was a police officer sitting near us having ice cream, and a call came in over his radio. We heard that your pie shop had been broken into, and we were terribly worried about you. We came here right away."

Theo nodded. "And I just happened to be walking up to the ice-cream parlor when they were running away. I asked them what was wrong, and when they told me, I wanted to come check on you, too. What happened here? Who would do this?"

I sighed. "I wish I knew. I'm assuming it was whoever ran me off the road, and whoever killed Tom. But who that actually is, well...your guess is as good as mine."

Molly's eyes were full of fear. "Izzy, please, stop trying to chase down clues on this. Let Mitch handle it. This person is determined to stop you from finding out who they are, and I'm afraid they're going to kill you before you catch them."

I chewed my lower lip again, unsure of what to say. I couldn't deny that Molly was right. And with Mitch, Theo, and Scott all staring at me, concern filling their eyes, I felt like a fool for ever thinking I could take this case on.

"You're probably right," I admitted to Molly.

"I'm definitely right," she exclaimed. "And you're definitely not going home alone tonight. I'll come with you and stay at your house if you want, but I don't want to hear a single thing about how this isn't really that dangerous!"

I squirmed. "You really don't have to come stay with me. I could go to Grams' house, although I was a bit worried about getting her all riled up and worried at this time of night."

Molly shook her head back and forth emphatically. "No, don't worry your grandmother. I'll stay with you, and we'll have Sprinkles as well."

"I'll also post a patrol car outside your house for the night," Mitch interjected.

I looked up at him and shook my head. "Don't you think that's a bit of overkill? I don't want to take up a police officer's time for the entire night over my silly self."

Mitch frowned at me. "I don't think it's overkill. There's a murderer on the loose."

I let my shoulders slump slightly, whether from resignation or relief, I wasn't sure. One thing I knew though: if it made Mitch and Molly feel better to have a patrol officer outside my house, then I would let Mitch post one. After the way I'd acted tonight, I didn't feel that I had much of a right to protest. I owed them a bit of a concession.

"Alright. Molly can stay with me tonight, and I won't complain about the patrol officer."

The relief on all of their faces was obvious, and it only made me feel guiltier that I'd made everyone worry so much about me.

Besides, I had to admit that I'd been missing Molly. It would be nice to spend an evening with her. As she looped her arm through mine and we walked out of the pie shop together, I thought that for perhaps the first time that week, everything felt somewhat okay.

And yet, despite having my best friend close, and knowing that Mitch's officer would be watching out for me, I couldn't help but shiver at the realization that Tom's murderer was still out there on the loose—and still looking for me.

CHAPTER EIGHTEEN

Sprinkles and I made the drive home in silence, with Molly following in her car. I didn't even turn on the radio. Instead, I stared silently into the darkness ahead, wondering who was trying to get me and where they might be.

I tried not to think too much about how foolishly I had acted in ignoring Mitch and running to the pie shop. It had seemed like a good idea at the time, but the more I thought about it, the more I felt awful for the way that I had worried my friends.

The one bright spot in all of this was that Molly and I would finally get a chance to talk. I figured she'd already eaten dinner, but I knew I'd be able to convince her to eat a bite of pie and drink some wine with me. In fact, I had a brand new bottle open that I'd just started on before Mitch called. I smiled at the thought, but then the smile froze on my face as I remembered that I also had a pie in the oven—a pie that had now been baking for at least an hour longer than it should have been.

"Oh no!" I yelped as I threw the car into park in my driveway and got out to start running toward the door. Sprinkles barked at me, and I realized that I'd forgotten to let him out. Quickly, I opened the passenger door for him, then slammed it behind him as I resumed running to my front door. I heard Molly pulling into the driveway behind me, but I didn't turn around to look. My heart was sinking as I unlocked my front door and threw it open.

A horrible, burning smell greeted me, and I wrinkled up my nose.

"Gross!" I ran into the house and turned the oven off, but the damage was already done. When I opened the oven door, I saw a round block of what used to be pie. It was completely black and smoldering.

"Disgusting," I muttered. "Guess I'm not going to be taste-testing my first try of this Christmas pie."

"Izzy?" Molly's voice called from near my front entrance. "Are you alright? Why were you running so fast? And, *ugh*, what's that smell?"

I turned around as Molly came into my kitchen. "That smell is what used to be a spiked Christmas pie. I was testing recipes for my holiday menu when Mitch called to tell me about the break-in at the café. I forgot to turn the oven off as I was running out the door."

I started throwing open windows, and Molly frowned at me.

"Mitch wanted you to leave all the windows closed and locked tonight," she pointed out.

I glanced over my shoulder and raised an eyebrow at her. "Do you want to be in this house with no fresh air coming in right now?"

Molly shrugged in answer.

"That's what I thought," I said. "We'll only leave them open for a little bit until everything airs out. Besides, I see a patrol car pulling up right now. I don't think anyone's going to try to hurt me with a police officer parked right out front."

"I certainly hope not," Molly said as she began to help me in opening the windows. "Although, whoever this criminal is, they seem quite brazen. I can't believe they broke into your pie shop like that. It's not even that late, and Main Street wasn't exactly deserted. Anyone could have seen them."

"Yeah, but I don't think anyone did," I said sadly. "Which means we still don't know who they are. And I think the reason they broke in now instead of in the middle of the night is because they weren't after money or valuables. They were after me, and they were probably hoping that I would still be there, baking pies or closing up the shop."

"I guess," Molly said. "But it still seems strange to me. This person was smart enough to change the clues on a scavenger hunt, but not smart enough to realize that you aren't ever at the pie shop this late?"

I paused to consider this. I hadn't thought of that. "You're right. It is a bit strange." I shook my head and shrugged. "Who knows what they were thinking. I'm just glad they didn't seem to do any significant damage to anything in the cafe. I'll have to close down tomorrow, and maybe the next day. But within a day or two I should be able to get things repaired and be back in business."

"And then will you please leave this murder case alone?" Molly pleaded.

I hesitated. I knew what the right answer to this was. I knew that I should agree, and should let this case go. But still, it was hard for me to say the words out loud.

Molly let out a long, exasperated sigh. "Izzy, I'm not asking you to stop because I don't think you're capable, or because I don't want you to have any fun. You know that. And you know that I've been along for the ride with you while you were solving several other murder cases. But this case has proven to be especially dangerous, and none of us want to see you get hurt. Besides, we've all been constantly worried sick about you since someone tried to run you off the road. Is that really what you want? For all your friends to be constantly worried about you?"

"No," I said slowly. "Of course I don't want you to be worried sick about me. But it's hard to stop thinking about this case. It's totally consumed my mind."

Molly leaned against the island in my kitchen and sighed again. "It's okay to think about it, but maybe just talk to Mitch about your theories when you think of something instead of trying to chase down clues yourself. Please. Just let this one go."

As guilty as I felt, I still wasn't ready to commit to letting it go. But I didn't want to argue with Molly about it anymore, so I changed the subject.

"I'll think about it. But hey, since you're here, wasn't there something you wanted to talk to me about? We might as well chat now. In fact, I've already got a bottle of wine open."

I half expected Molly to tell me that I wasn't getting off that easily without promising to let Tom's murder case drop. But to my surprise, Molly didn't say anything more about the murder case. Instead, her cheeks turned bright red and she looked down at her hands.

"Yes, we should talk. But you might want to pour us a couple glasses of wine first." She gestured toward the open wine bottle, which sat a few feet away from her.

"Okay, sure," I said slowly. I was happy to share my wine with Molly, but I was worried that she seemed to think wine was necessary for whatever conversation we were about to have. "This sounds serious."

"It is serious," Molly said, then hurried to add "Not *bad* serious, but, well…"

I slid a glass of wine over to her and cocked my head quizzically. "Just spit it out."

Molly nodded, took a deep breath, and then said, "Scott and I are dating."

I nearly choked on the sip of wine I'd just taken, and my eyes widened as I stared at Molly for several speechless moments.

"What?!? Really?"

Molly nodded, seeming to feel better now that she'd said her secret out loud. "It's true. We only officially decided to date two weeks ago, but things have been going really well. I know it probably sounds crazy to you, because I was always so set on chasing a rich guy with a lot of money who could support my dreams of luxury. And we all know Scott isn't exactly rich. But one night a few weeks ago when Scott and I were at dinner by ourselves because you couldn't make it, we realized that we actually have quite a bit in common. We started talking about our dreams and hopes for the future, and we realized that we are actually kind of perfect for each other."

I blinked at Molly, still not quite sure what to say.

Molly filled the gap in the conversation. "Honestly, it's been so great. Dating someone who has been such a good friend has made the whole process feel so easy and comfortable. I'm having the time of my life. I know it might seem a bit awkward at first since Scott and you and me have been a platonic trio for so long. And I know I'd be a fool to say this won't change anything. But I promise it won't change much. We'll still all be good friends, and, well, I'm just hoping that you can be happy for me."

For several more moments I remained speechless. I hadn't had a clue what Molly wanted to talk about, but the idea that it would be that she was dating someone—let alone that that someone was Scott—had never crossed my mind.

Finally, after I stared at her for several moments, Molly bit her lower lip and said, "Izzy, please say something."

"I don't know what to say." I could feel a surge of anger starting to grow within me. "Why didn't you tell me sooner?"

To my surprise, I saw anger in Molly's eyes as well. "When was I supposed to tell you? I wanted to tell you in person, but you've been too busy over the last few weeks to meet with me. When you're not at your café, you're off chasing down a murderer."

Molly slammed her fist down in frustration before continuing. "You know you're my best friend and that I care deeply about you, but lately you seem to be getting more and more selfish and caring less and less about spending time with your friends."

I swallowed hard, not sure what to say. Molly paced a few more moments, then kept ranting.

"I've been terrified that someone would realize Scott and I were dating and that you would hear about it through the gossip mill. We tried to be careful, and it was fairly easy not to raise anyone's suspicions since Scott and I have hung out as friends for a long time, anyway. Most people who saw us together probably didn't suspect that our relationship had changed. But still, you know how things are here. Someone would have eventually figured it out, and I just wanted to tell you in person before that happened. But you've been declining all my requests to talk. Don't try to deny it. You know it's true."

Molly crossed her arms and glared at me. I wasn't sure I'd ever seen her truly angry, and for a moment, I was tempted to cross my arms and be angry right back. But I forced myself to pause, take a few deep breaths, and really listen to what Molly was saying.

She was right. She had been trying to meet with me, and I'd been continuously brushing her off.

As I stood there in the middle of my kitchen, I realized that I'd been quite wrapped up in myself over the last few months. True, it had been a hard time in my life. I was coming off of a nasty divorce, and I was desperately trying to make my café successful. There had been a lot on my mind, and the murder cases I'd worked on had been a welcome distraction from the grind of eking out a new life here in Sunshine Springs.

But I had become too distracted and too self-centered. I couldn't argue with Molly. It was my own fault that she hadn't told me yet about her and Scott.

I took a deep breath and forced myself to look her in the eye.

"You're right. I'm sorry. I haven't been around much, and I'm embarrassed to say that I haven't exactly been a good friend. I promise I'll do better. And I'm really happy for you and Scott. Truly." I smiled. "I have to say, I *had* noticed that he was flirting a lot less with me over the last few weeks."

That got a laugh from Molly. Scott had always flirted with both of us incessantly, and we had both insisted that we would never date him because he was just a friend. Apparently, though, he had convinced Molly that he was worth having a relationship with after all.

"I'm really happy that you're not mad that I'm dating him," Molly said. "You're *not* mad, right? I didn't want you to feel like I was stealing him from you or anything."

It was my turn to laugh. "Of course I'm not mad. Scott's totally not my type, even if he was fun to flirt with sometimes. But now that I think about it, I can really see how you two would go well together. I'm truly happy for you. The only thing I'll say is that if for some reason things don't work out between you two, you better not become enemies. I don't want to have to be in the middle of any fights."

Molly smiled, her cheeks turning pink again. "I'll do my best not to become enemies with him," she said with a laugh. "And I know it's early to say, but I feel like this might really be a long-term relationship. I'm really happy." She beamed as she looked up at me, and I smiled back at her.

"Well then, I'm happy for you." Then I winked at her. "And Theo and Mitch will be happy to know that they have one less competitor for my attention."

Molly laughed. "You should hurry up and choose one of them so that we can go on double dates. That would be so fun!"

I laughed too, but then shook my head. "You know I'm not interested in dating right now. And even though Mitch and Theo are good friends to me, I'm not sure I'll ever be interested in dating them. After how badly my last marriage went, I'm not sure I have the guts to try again."

This was true. At one point a few months ago I had almost caved and started dating Theo. But life had intervened, and I had decided that I'd rather keep both Mitch and Theo as friends, even though I knew both of them would have dated me in a heartbeat. Now, I sincerely hoped that both of them would find a good girl who would make them happy. True, I was flattered that they seemed to be waiting around for me to make up my mind to date one of them. But they deserved to be happy, and I wasn't the best person to make either of them happy.

For now, I kept the conversation focused on Molly. "You and Scott are the perfect combo. I can't believe I never really saw it before."

Molly grinned. "Thanks. I'm happy that you know now, so I don't have to keep worrying that someone's going to figure it out before I have the chance to tell you."

I felt another pang of guilt. "I'm really sorry again, for everything. I promise I'll do better."

Molly was still smiling, apparently happy just to have had the chance to talk to me. But she did furrow her brow and give me a long, hard look. "And will you promise to leave this murder case alone? I'm not saying you have to give up all sleuthing for all time. But please, just let Mitch handle this one so I can stop worrying so much about you."

I took a deep breath. I didn't want to give up this case, but I felt that I owed Molly and the rest of my friends this much. They'd been so patient with me, and they were right. It was dangerous, and I was being selfish by putting myself in danger over and over just so that I could be the one to solve this case. It was time to let it go.

I took a deep breath and nodded. "Okay. If it means that much to you, then I'll leave this case alone."

"Really?" The smile on Molly's face told me that I was making the right decision.

"Really," I said. "So enough talk about that. I want to hear all about you and Scott. I really am so happy for you. And I hope you have a lot to tell, because we're going to be here in this kitchen for a while. I need to try to make another one of these Christmas pies since the first one went so horribly wrong."

Molly practically glowed. "I can't wait to tell you everything. I've been bursting at the seams to tell you all about our dates. It really has been like a fairytale."

I smiled at my friend, happy to see her so happy. I knew she'd been searching for love for a long time. From the way she was talking, she'd realized that her Prince Charming was right under her nose, and I wanted to hear all about how her fairytale was going.

But as I started to remove the horribly burnt pie from the baking dish so that I could start prepping a new pie, Molly held up her hand.

"Wait, before you do that, let's take a selfie."

I frowned at her. "A selfie? With a burnt pie?"

Molly grinned at me. "Yes, with a burnt pie. We haven't taken a selfie together in ages, and this would be a fun one."

I shook my head at her. "You're a weirdo, you know that? Who wants to take a selfie with a burnt pie?"

Of course, I already knew the answer to that question: Molly, that's who. Molly loved to take selfies, and she had a whole album on her social media account of the most unique selfies she could come up with. I thought she was a bit crazy for wanting one with the burnt pie, but I humored her as she held her cell phone out in front of her and told me to smile for the camera.

A few hours later, I collapsed into bed, exhausted but happy. Molly had told me all about how happy she was with Scott, and it was good to see my friend so happy.

I was happy, too. I'd baked several spiked Christmas pies, and I was happy with how the recipe seemed to be working, which meant I'd made a step forward in my holiday menu planning.

The burnt smell had faded from my house, so I closed and locked all the windows and doors. With Molly here, I wasn't alone, and I did feel better knowing there was a police officer right outside. Even though I was frustrated by the break-in at the café, the day had ended on a good note, after all.

As I collapsed into bed, I grabbed my phone to quickly scroll through my social media accounts. Beside me, Sprinkles whined. He hated the light from my phone, and I knew I should probably be going straight to sleep instead of wasting time online. But I couldn't resist a few minutes of mindless browsing.

When I opened my phone's social media apps, though, I immediately saw that Molly had posted the selfie of her and me next to the blackened, burnt pie. I rolled my eyes, but my heart warmed when I read the caption she'd posted along with the photo.

Even when things don't go as planned, there's no better feeling in the world than hanging out with your best friend.

"No better feeling, indeed," I murmured with a smile. I set my phone down on my nightstand and closed my eyes to drift off into happy sleep. For once, I'd ended the day on a good note with my friends, and I fully intended to keep my promise to Molly to leave Tom's murder case alone. I just hoped that the murderer would get the memo that I was no longer sleuthing, and would leave me alone in return.

But I had a feeling that whoever was after me wasn't going to give up quite so easily.

CHAPTER NINETEEN

The next morning, Molly had a quick breakfast with me before leaving for her job at the library. She'd been quite busy over the last few months in her job as head librarian, since the library had been given a windfall from the estate of one of Sunshine Springs' residents who had recently passed away. Molly had been busy overseeing remodels and new book purchases for the library, and I'd never seen her quite as happy as she was right then. Now that she and I had cleared the air and were on good terms again, everything seemed to be perfect for her. She had her perfect guy, her perfect job, and, dare I say it, a perfect best friend.

I giggled at this thought as I watched her drive away. I knew I wasn't perfect, of course. But I liked to think that, for the most part, my good qualities outweighed my bad.

Today, I was especially determined to showcase my good side. I still felt guilty over the way I'd ignored Mitch last night, and I determined that the best thing to do would be to go apologize to him in person with a freshly baked pie. No matter how angry Mitch was with me, he could never stay angry when I brought him pie. He loved my baking, and that was lucky for me, because I seemed to have a knack for pushing his buttons and irritating him.

I felt confident that he wouldn't be able to stay irritated with me today. Not when I had other news for him that would make him happy: I would let him know that I'd promised Molly to let this murder case go. He would definitely be relieved to hear that.

Before I left to see Mitch, I checked in with Ruby to let her know there was no need for her to come in for her shift at the café today. When I called her, I half-expected her to already know about the break-in. The story must have been making the rounds like lightning through the Sunshine Springs gossip chain. But to my surprise, Ruby didn't know.

"Are you serious?" she asked, shock in her voice. "I can't believe someone would do such a thing!"

She asked me if anything had been stolen, and if I was okay. I appreciated her concern, but I tried to keep the conversation brief. I wasn't in the mood to rehash everything that had happened. It was bad enough that I was sure I'd have to give a detailed account to my insurance company when I called them later today. For now, I just wanted to focus on positive things.

Positive things like taking spiked Christmas pie to Sheriff Mitch McCoy.

When I arrived at the police station, the receptionist didn't look all that surprised to see me.

"Here to give a statement?" she asked.

It occurred to me then that I'd given a ridiculous number of statements here at the police station over my brief time in Sunshine Springs. I always seemed to be tangled up in the town's latest drama. But today, thankfully, I wasn't here to give a statement.

"No, but I would like to talk to Mitch if he's available? I brought him some pie."

The receptionist sniffed appreciatively. "Is that a new recipe? It doesn't smell like anything you've brought in before."

"Yup, it's new. A potential addition to my Christmas menu."

The receptionist grinned. "Well, if it tastes as good as it smells, then you should definitely put it on your Christmas menu. I'll have to make sure I swipe a piece from Mitch later. Hang on. I'll see if he's available."

The receptionist picked up her phone and called Mitch's office. A few moments later Mitch himself appeared in the entryway wearing a skeptical look on his face.

"Morning, Izzy." He sounded and looked exhausted, and I felt another pang of guilt as I realized that he'd likely been worrying about me last night. He glanced dubiously at the pie box. "If you think you can just bring pie to butter me up and make me forget the fact that you won't leave this case alone, then you're not as smart as I thought you were."

I put a hand on my hip and gave him an exaggeratedly innocent look. "What? Me? Bribe someone with pie? I would never!"

Mitch rolled his eyes at me, no doubt thinking of the many times before that I'd bribed him with pie. He gestured for me to follow him down the hall.

"If you want to talk to me then come on back. But I'm not going to be okay with your sticking your nose in this case just because you brought me pie. This whole thing is too dangerous, and I'm constantly worried about you."

I followed him to his office without another word, waiting until we were both seated and I had opened the pie box to begin my apology.

"Listen, I didn't come here to try to bribe you with pie so that you'd stop telling me not to work on this case. Quite the opposite, in fact. I wanted to let you know that I promised Molly last night that I would leave this case alone."

For several beats, Mitch just stared at me, as though waiting for the punch line. Finally, I couldn't take it anymore and I threw my hands up in the air in exasperation. "I'm serious! I'm really giving up the case. That's what you wanted, isn't it?"

Mitch still looked uncertain. "Yes, it's what I wanted. But I never expected you to actually do it. You're really serious? You're really giving up the case?"

I nodded. "I'm giving up the case. And to prove to you that I'm serious about this, I'm here to tell you everything that I know so far about the case. You know that I don't usually like to give up my clues, but since I'm not going to be chasing down any clues on this anymore, I figured it was time to tell you what I know."

Mitch leaned forward expectantly, not able to hide his excitement. For a moment, I thought about teasing him and telling him that he seemed to think I was a good detective after all. But I bit my tongue. Mitch had never said that I wasn't a good detective. He'd just said that this was all too dangerous for me. Besides, I didn't want to ruin my apology by irritating him with my teasing. Instead, I took a deep breath and launched into my explanation of everything that I'd heard about Belinda and Sophia. First, I told him about Sophia's strange conversation that made it sound like she had been in some sort of bad real estate dealings with Tom.

Mitch was as surprised as I had been to hear that. "I never would have pegged Sophia as the type to be irresponsible or take big risks with her money."

He didn't say it, but I knew that he was probably also thinking the same thing I had thought when I first learned about Sophia's money troubles: if Sophia had acted in ways we didn't think she would with her money, then who was to say that she hadn't also acted in ways we didn't think she would when it came to committing murder? Sure, it still felt like quite a bit of a stretch to think that Sophia had been the one to kill Tom, but it worried me at least a little bit that she had acted so out of character when it came to money.

From the look on Mitch's face, it worried him, too. I didn't dwell too long on that point, though. I would let Mitch draw his own conclusions. For now, I continued on with telling him that I'd overheard Belinda talking about how she and Tom had been having trouble.

"I don't know if it really means that much," I said. "After all, it's a big jump from someone having trouble in their relationship to someone murdering their significant other. But I thought I'd mention it just in case."

Mitch nodded thoughtfully, then frowned at me. "Do I even want to know how you came by all of this information?"

I felt my cheeks heating up. I knew Mitch wouldn't appreciate the fact that I'd snuck into Belinda's and Sophia's yards to peer into their houses and spy on them. So, I just smiled at him a bit ruefully and shook my head.

"It's probably better if you don't ask."

Mitch sighed. "I was afraid of that. I'm just glad that you've agreed not to do anymore of whatever it is you've been doing. Is there anything else you want to tell me?"

I shook my head. "No, that's about it. And please, now that you know that I'm going to stay out of things, why don't you relax and eat a little bit of pie? I would actually love to know what your thoughts are on this flavor. It's a spiked Christmas pie that I'm planning to add to my holiday menu."

Mitch raised an eyebrow. "Christmas pie already? It's only just September."

"I know. But trust me: the holiday season comes up faster than you think. You have to be prepared for it, or it catches you off guard and you miss out on a lot of holiday sales."

"I see," Mitch said as he picked up a plastic fork that I'd put in the pie box for him. He didn't even bother cutting a slice with the plastic pie cutter. Instead, he dug right in, loading his fork with a huge bite of pie and shoving it into his mouth. He chewed thoughtfully for a few moments, then grinned at me. "Yup. This one's definitely a keeper. If you add it to your holiday menu then you'll get lots of holiday sales for sure."

I beamed. "You really think so?"

"I know so," Mitch said as he reached for another forkful. "In fact, I'd stake my career on it. And you know I don't say that lightly. My career means everything to me."

"I know that all too well. But don't worry. I'll be staying out of your way and letting you handle things with this murder case, so you can be the one to get a boost for your career when this thing is solved."

Mitch's face turned serious. "Thank you, Izzy. That really means a lot to me. I know it's not easy for you to give this up, but I really am going to sleep so much better at night knowing that you're not out there sticking your nose in danger."

I smiled at him. "You're right. This definitely isn't easy for me. But I know it's the right thing to do. And I really am sorry for the way I acted. It wasn't right of me to make so many people worry just because I couldn't contain my own curiosity. But, if you don't mind, I do have one favor to ask."

Mitch instantly looked suspicious. "What's that?"

I smiled at him. "Don't worry. It's nothing major. I would just really appreciate it if you would let me know when you do solve the case. I'm still really curious, and you can't blame me for being a little bit concerned, can you? After all, I've had a couple attempts on my life now. You're not the only one who will breathe easier once this is all solved."

Mitch nodded. "Don't worry. When I solve this thing, you'll be the first one to know."

I let out a relieved breath, then stood to go. "Well, in that case, I won't take up any more of your time. I know you've got a lot of work to do. Please, enjoy that pie. But make sure you give a slice to your receptionist. She was quite curious about how it would taste."

Mitch smiled at me. "I'll definitely give her a piece. But only a small one. I want to keep most of this pie for myself."

I laughed as I slung my purse over my shoulder and turned toward the door. "Fair enough."

"Wait," Mitch said. "What are you going to do today? Work on fixing up your pie shop?"

I paused and turned back toward him. "Yeah. I'll have to call some repair people to come fix the windows and doors, and I'll have to talk to my insurance company about making a claim. But what I'm actually going to do right now is head over to Sophia's salon."

Mitch narrowed his eyes at me. "So, you promised me you're staying out of things and then you go to the hair salon owned by one of the main suspects?"

I shrugged. "It's hard for me to believe that Sophia actually had anything to do with this. But even if she did, she's not going to hurt me in the middle of her salon with so many people around. And I promise I won't try to get any clues or information out of her. I just thought that the salon was a good, safe place to be. It's always full of people, so I won't be alone. Besides, Grams texted me and told me she's changing her hair to turquoise today. She asked if I wanted to spend some time at the salon and hang out with her, and I can't resist. I've seen Grams with a lot of different colors of hair, but I think turquoise is a new one."

Mitch laughed. "Okay, then. You're right. The salon probably is a safe place for you to be. Just be careful, and don't hesitate to call if you feel threatened in any way by anything. Even if it seems like a small thing that's only in your head, I want to know about it. Better to be safe than sorry."

I nodded at him. "Of course. I'll keep you posted if I am worried about anything. In the meantime, enjoy your pie."

"I intend to," Mitch said as I gave him a small wave and disappeared into the hallway.

I felt lighter already. Yes, it made me a little sad to give up working on this case. But knowing that my friends had been so worried about me, and that I was now doing what I could to ease those worries, I felt better. I felt like I was actually doing what I could to be a good friend, and that mattered to me. Perhaps I had forgotten just how much it mattered in the chaos of the last several months, but I was determined to do better and to be as good of a friend to my friends as they had been to me.

With a skip in my step, I headed out to Grams' car. I would pick her up and we'd go to Sophia's salon together. I'd already spoken to a rental car company, and they were going to bring a rental car to the salon for me so that when I left later this afternoon I wouldn't have to take Grams' car again.

I took a deep breath, and my smile widened as I pulled out onto the road. It was going to be a good day. I would be spending time with Grams, and I could relax. Once I took care of getting a repairman out to the pie shop, I didn't have to do anything except enjoy my spa treatments. I would be safe, too. Whoever wanted to hurt me wouldn't do so in the middle of Sophia's Snips.

At least, that's what I told myself as I drove. But when you know there's a murderer on the loose who wants to take you out, it's not easy to keep yourself from constantly looking over your shoulder.

CHAPTER TWENTY

Grams didn't say much on the ride over, but I talked quite a bit. I told her about all of the clues I'd discovered surrounding Tom's murder, and I told her how I'd agreed not to pursue this case anymore, and she had nodded approvingly.

"Usually, I don't like to tell you to give up," she'd said. "But I think that this is one of those circumstances where it's the wiser thing to do. Mitch will handle it. He's good at this sort of thing, and he's got his whole police force backing him. He'll get it figured out, and keep you and Sunshine Springs safe. Besides, don't feel like you're completely giving up. You've found a few clues, haven't you? You found the hairclip, and you found out that Belinda was on the outs with Tom. That's something."

I shrugged. "It's something, but not much. I don't know that anything will come of either the hairclips or Belinda's problems with Tom. Those things both sound like they might have just been coincidence."

I hadn't told Grams about Sophia's money troubles at all. I still couldn't bring myself to say out loud to Grams that everyone's favorite hairdresser might have a darker side. In fact, I still didn't want to believe it myself, although the further I got into this case, the more I couldn't see how anyone else was looking guiltier than Sophia.

Still, the pieces didn't quite fit right for accusing Sophia, and I didn't want to get Grams upset for nothing. I couldn't help but feeling like there was something more to this than Sophia or Belinda, even though I had no solid proof of that. It was just a hunch, and hunches weren't good evidence. Besides, I was done with this case. I'd turned it over completely to Mitch, and I was sure he didn't want to hear about my hunches.

Sophia's Snips was busy, but not overwhelmingly so. It had been a while since I'd been here on an ordinary weekday, when there was no special gossip going on and no holiday events coming up for which everyone wanted their hair done. I hadn't made an appointment, but Sophia waved me in and told me she'd squeeze me in for whatever I wanted if I could be patient enough.

Being patient wouldn't be a problem. I had all day. On the way to pick up Grams, I had made some phone calls. The repairman was on his way to fix the broken window and door at my pie shop, and I'd deal with the insurance company later. For now, I wanted to get things fixed so that I could reopen tomorrow.

I especially didn't want Ruby to miss too many shifts. If she started thinking that the pie shop might be closed any old day because of a break-in or a murder, I was going to lose her as an employee, and I couldn't afford to lose an employee right now. The tourist season might be winding down, but I needed help at the café so that I'd have time to get ready for the holiday season.

Ruby had already texted me a few times asking for updates on the repairs. I got the feeling that she wasn't happy about missing her shift today, although she had been gracious enough about it. Still, I didn't want to push my luck. I did my best to keep her updated throughout the day, in hopes that for now at least that would be enough. I tried to push my worries away as I walked into the salon.

Grams, who had an appointment, went to sit at the chair of one of Sophia's employees. Sprinkles, who had been patiently coming along with me for the ride all morning, now went to sit happily by Grams. The only thing that seemed to make Sprinkles happier than the times that I agreed to give him slices of pie were the times that Grams brought him to the salon.

Of course, today *I* was technically the one who had brought him here, but he didn't seem to care. This was his special place with Grams, and he sat faithfully by her as Sophia's employee began to work on her hair.

After I'd been sitting for a few minutes, casually flipping through a magazine and half-listening to the chatter in the salon, Sophia finished up with her current client and asked what I would like done.

I reached up and touched my hair. I didn't really need a hair service, but my nails were looking a bit sad. I held them up for Sophia to see.

"How about a manicure?"

Sophia beamed at me. "Coming right up. I'll squeeze you in with one of the nail techs."

At the mention of a manicure, Sprinkles' ears perked up and he left his post by Grams to come investigate. I wasn't sure whether to laugh or roll my eyes.

"What's up, Sprinkles?" I asked him. "You want a manicure, too?"

He woofed in reply, and Sophia looked up at me with a grin. "I guess I'll make that two manicures, then?"

I sighed. "I guess so. Although, technically Sprinkles will be getting a pedicure."

Sprinkles wagged his tail at me, clearly excited by the fact that he was about to get his nails painted. Ever since I moved to Sunshine Springs, Grams had been bringing him here with her every time she came to the salon, which was at least once a week—often more. And every time she brought him, she treated him to a pedicure and got his nails painted.

The first time she'd done it, I hadn't been able to believe that she had taken my boy Dalmatian and had his toenails painted. But now, I expected it. Any time that Grams petsat Sprinkles for me, I knew he'd be coming back with a fresh coat of polish on his toenails. Although he'd been wary at first, he now seemed to enjoy his pedicures just as much as Grams enjoyed getting them for him.

From across the room, Grams chuckled, and then teased me. "I knew you'd come around and see that Sprinkles deserves a good pedicure now and then."

"Now and then?" I said, taking on an overly incredulous tone just to tease Grams right back. "Seems to me that this dog gets his nails done more often than I do."

Grams raised a playful finger in my direction. "It's not his fault that you don't pay attention to the state of your nails. It's no wonder you don't have a man, with nails that look like that."

"Grams!" I exclaimed. "I can't believe you said that! The reason I don't have a man is because I don't want one right now. You know that."

I felt my face heating up with embarrassment, and I wondered what had gotten into Grams. It wasn't like her to discuss my love life, especially not in front of everyone at Sophia's Snips. The other ladies in the salon stared down at their magazines and pretended not to hear, but I knew they were listening.

"I'm just saying," Grams said. "After you get your nails painted here you should go out on the town a bit and show them off for once. In fact, why don't you head down to Theo's winery and wave those nails in his direction? He'd be a good catch, don't you think?"

I glared at Grams even harder. She knew that Theo had an interest in me, and I could see now exactly what she was trying to do. She thought that if she got the town talking about Theo and me that it would ratchet up the pressure for me to actually date him. But I wasn't going to fall for her schemes. I smiled sweetly at her, made no reply, and turned my attention to Sprinkles.

"What do you think, boy?" I asked him. "What colors should we choose?"

He looked at Grams and barked, and I laughed. "You want your nails to match Grams' hair?"

He barked again, wagging his tail wildly.

"Alright, then," I said as I scanned the shelves of nail polish for a bottle that matched the turquoise hue that was slowly being applied to Grams' hair. I found one that was close enough, and smiled at Sprinkles. "Let's both do this color. Then we'll all match."

Sprinkles barked excitedly, and a few minutes later he and I were both enjoying a spa treatment—his for his toenails, and mine for my fingernails.

That was when I finally started to truly relax. Grams was right: I often didn't take good care of myself. Between the pie shop and my sleuthing, my friends weren't the only thing I hadn't had time for. I had neglected my own well-being, and as I sat there having coconut-scented lotion rubbed into my hands, I determined that I was going to make more time for things like this. It felt good to relax for once.

Conversation buzzed around me, although I didn't participate much myself at the moment. I sat and enjoyed listening to everyone around me catching up on what was going on in Sunshine Springs. I smiled as I realized that no one was talking about Molly and Scott yet. I knew it would be only a short time before someone would catch on, and the whole town would be whispering for a while about how Molly and Scott were a thing. Eventually, interest in their relationship would fade, and the gossip would move on to the next new couple or some other scandal.

There wasn't any chatter about Tom's murder, which surprised me a little bit. But when I thought about it, I realized that nobody wanted to talk about it in front of Sophia. I didn't blame them. Nobody, myself included, wanted to believe that she was guilty. And she seemed so happy right now that I figured that no one wanted to ruin that happiness by bringing up the case.

In fact, Sophia almost seemed like her normal self, laughing and fluttering her fingers occasionally as she shared her viewpoint on this or that piece of town gossip. I noticed that she looked a little less emaciated than the last time I'd seen her, which made me wonder if her loan had gone through. Perhaps she now had money to buy groceries again. There were still bags under her eyes, but they didn't look as bad as before. Perhaps the worst of the whole situation was behind her—assuming of course that murdering Tom hadn't been part of that situation. But as I looked at her now, I couldn't see how anyone would possibly believe that it had been her. She was just too sweet, too full of life, and too full of laughter for anyone to think it had been her.

Unless she was working hard to put on a good show to cover up the fact that she'd killed Tom.

I shook my head as I thought through all of this. I wasn't supposed to be working on this case anymore. Perhaps there was no harm in considering the suspects, but it was hard for me to consider things without wanting to jump into seeking out clues again, and I had promised Mitch that I wouldn't do that. I had to get my mind on something else.

Luckily, one of the little old ladies in the salon sat down beside me at that moment to get a manicure. She seemed interested in talking to me, and I knew she wouldn't want to talk about the murder with Sophia standing nearby, so a conversation with her was sure to help me keep my mind off of things.

I looked over and gave her a broad smile. "Good morning, Rose. How have you been?"

"Oh, I've been all right, dear. You know how it is when you get older, I'm sure, since you spend so much time with your Grams. You try to keep your head up as much as possible, but it's not always easy when you're old and achy."

I didn't bother to mention to her that Grams never acted old and achy. In fact, I thought Grams probably acted less old and achy than many women half her age. But that wasn't what Rose wanted to hear, so I smiled sympathetically at her and nodded. "Well, I'm glad to hear that you're hanging in there. Hopefully this heat wave will be over soon, and that will make things easier on you."

Rose nodded sagely. "Very true, very true. This heat has been tough on me." Then she wagged a finger playfully at me. "And it was made tougher by the fact that the last time I tried to go get a nice slice of cool lemon vodka pie from your café, you were closed."

I frowned at her in confusion. "Did you go this morning?"

It was early in the day, and if Rose had gone to my cafe before coming here, it would have been a bit early in the day for lemon vodka pie. But I didn't judge my customers. If they wanted vodka pie at nine in the morning, then that's what I would give them. The customer was always right, after all.

But Rose was shaking her head. "Oh, no, dear. Not this morning. Yesterday, and the day before that. I went by in the afternoon and there was a closed sign on the door even though it wasn't time for the pie shop to be closed yet. I just assumed that maybe you didn't have enough help. I know you hired that Ruby girl recently, and she seems like she's been working out well for you. But I know it must still be hard with only one employee."

I frowned, more confused than ever. "The pie shop was closed? Really? I thought Ruby was there all afternoon."

Rose was shaking her head. "No, when I stopped by the café it was closed. But perhaps she was taking a break, and I just happened to be there at the wrong moment."

Rose shrugged, then moved on to a different topic of conversation. I smiled and nodded as she started talking about her plans for the upcoming fall festival, but I only half-heard what she was saying.

I couldn't help but feel a bit irritated. Ruby had actually closed the pie shop? I didn't necessarily blame her if she had. I knew the shop got busy, and she was still a new employee learning how to handle everything. If she'd needed to take a break, I would have understood. But it irritated me that she hadn't mentioned anything to me about a break. She'd implied that she'd kept the pie shop open the entire time I'd been gone. True, she'd never actually said that, but she'd certainly let me think it.

Rose paused just then and seemed to notice my irritation. "Is everything alright, dear?"

I forced a smile onto my face. "Yes, everything's fine. I just have a lot on my mind. Sorry if I was frowning. Keep telling me about your quilts that you're going to enter in the festival's quilting contest. They sound lovely."

Rose beamed, and continued on with the description of the quilts. But she trailed off when she heard Sophia starting to sniffle. I looked over, too, surprised to see that Sophia's happy demeanor had once again disappeared, and tears were glistening in her eyes. I also saw that Grams was shaking her head, and reaching over to pat Sophia's hand. Slowly, the other women from the salon were gathering around her as well.

"What's going on?" I asked Rose.

"I'm not sure," Rose replied. "I wasn't listening. But something is definitely wrong with Sophia."

The whole salon seemed to hold its breath as Sophia sobbed quietly. Eventually, she looked up and said in an angry voice, "I just can't believe that he would tell anyone that! Did he think I was joking when I said I wouldn't give him my business if he blabbed my business to everyone?"

"Don't be so upset," Grams said soothingly. "We all go through hard times financially. It's nothing to be ashamed of."

I perked up. Had the banker leaked the information about Sophia's financial troubles to the town? Beside me, Rose was just as eager to figure out what was going on.

"Kathy," she said to another woman on her right side. "What's this all about?"

Kathy looked over. "Apparently, Sophia did some bad real estate deals with Tom. That got her in a lot of financial trouble, and she needed to get a loan to dig herself out of it. She got one from Harold down at the Sunshine Springs Bank, but she made him promise not to tell anyone because she felt like it would ruin her reputation if we all knew she had financial problems."

Rose frowned. "Really? Doesn't everyone have financial problems now and then?"

Kathy shrugged. "Of course. But I guess Sophia had this made out to be a much bigger deal in her head than it really was. Anyway, someone asked her just now about her financial troubles, so I guess the secret is out."

I watched as Sophia suddenly stood, marched across the room, and picked up the phone. Right there in the middle of her shop, she called the bank and asked to speak to the banker who had been working on the loan with her. We all sat, mesmerized, as she began yelling at him. Whatever he was saying only seemed to make her angrier.

"I know it was you!" Sophia yelled. "I haven't even finalized the loan yet, and no one else knew about it. It had to have been you, so don't try to deny it! And don't think that I'm going to go through with this now! You've lost my business!"

Sophia slammed the phone down, and an awkward silence hung in the room. I squirmed uncomfortably in my seat, realizing that it wasn't exactly true that no one else had known about the loan. I had known, although the only reason was because I'd been spying on Sophia. Was it possible someone else had been spying on her, too? Mitch knew, too, since I'd told him this morning. But there was no way he would have said anything to anyone. That meant that if the banker indeed hadn't been the one to tell—and why would he have, when he didn't even have the loan finalized yet—then someone else was on Sophia's trail.

But who? And why?

My heart started to pound with excitement, and as if he could sense it, Sprinkles looked over at me and whined. He put a paw on my knee, and I glanced down at his black and white spotted fur that was now accented by bright turquoise toenails.

"I know, I know," I said to him softly. "I'm not supposed to be worrying about clues."

And really, I was trying my best to stay out of things. I couldn't help it if all of this drama kept landing in my lap. Perhaps I should just go home after all, and stay away from everyone until this blew over. Sophia had started ranting once again about how awful the banker was for telling her business to everyone when he'd sworn he wouldn't. But then Kathy, the woman on the other side of Rose, shook her head and spoke up.

"Are you quite sure it was him? Is there anyone else who might have known?"

Sophia looked over, sniffling in anger. "It had to have been him. I hadn't told anyone else.

Kathy shrugged. "I only asked because it seems to me that sometimes secrets in this town take on a life of their own. They get out without anyone actually telling them."

Sophia frowned. "What do you mean?"

Kathy shrugged. "I only mean that you're not the only one whose secrets have inexplicably come to light. Everyone knows how I'm stepping down from the City Council, but I never told anyone that except my husband. I wasn't planning to announce it until I actually stepped down, but when I went to the Morning Brew Café for coffee this morning, everyone already knew."

Sophia sniffled, starting to look more curious than angry. "Then your husband must have told someone."

Kathy shook her head. "I don't think so. He was still trying to convince me not to step down, so I don't think he would have gone around blabbing to everyone that that was my plan. Anyway, all I'm saying is that it seems secrets have a way of getting out in this town, even when you do your darndest to keep them secret."

Kathy shrugged in resignation, then went back to reading her magazine. For a few moments, the only sound I could hear was the bubbling water around Kathy's feet as she soaked them in preparation for a pedicure. As I watched her, she absentmindedly reached up and touched her hairclip, adjusting it and sweeping some stray strands of hair back behind her ear.

I frowned, realizing that this was the same type of blue, sparkly hairclip that had been at the burnt lemon grove, at my café after the break-in, and in Grams' hair. I flashed back to this morning, when I'd been sitting in Mitch's office, apologizing to him and giving him pie. One of those blue hairclips had been sitting on a shelf in his office.

As I looked around now, I saw that several women were wearing the hairclips.

That's when a crazy, ridiculous idea occurred to me. I knew I wasn't supposed to be working on this case, but this idea was too exciting and too all-consuming for me to push it away completely. I had to check on something, and I couldn't wait another moment to do so. If I was right, I would take the clue directly to Mitch, but I had to see for sure right this minute.

I hopped out of my chair, not caring that I was in the middle of a manicure. At least the nail tech hadn't put any polish on my hands yet, so it wasn't as though I was going to smudge anything.

"Sophia, do you have any more of those sparkly blue hairclips for sale?" I asked in a breathless voice.

Looking startled, Sophia nodded. "Sure, a few. Why?"

"Where are they? I need to buy one!"

Sophia frowned at me in confusion. So did Grams and everyone else.

"They're on the display over by the front register," Sophia said. "But why do you have to have one right this second? Don't you want to finish your manicure first?"

"Nope," I said, rushing over to the display. Sprinkles followed excitedly behind me, caught up in my enthusiasm.

"Izzy?" Grams asked in a tone of voice that said she thought I'd gone a bit off my rocker. "What are you doing?"

I didn't slow down as I reached the display of hairclips.

"I need to take a look at one of these hairclips. I think I know how all of these secrets in Sunshine Springs have been getting out."

CHAPTER TWENTY-ONE

As the entire hair salon watched, I grabbed one of the hairclips from the display, then grabbed the large, industrial telephone that sat on the front counter. I took a deep breath, then brought the phone down hard on top of the hairclip.

One of the women in the salon shrieked in surprise. Even Grams looked a little shocked, although she was used to my tendency to behave somewhat strangely at times.

"Izzy!" Grams exclaimed. "What in the world are you doing?"

I didn't answer right away. Instead, I set the phone aside and looked at the shattered hairclip. I pulled the pieces apart, brushing aside little shards of sparkly blue to see if I would find what I was looking for.

I did.

"Bingo!" I shouted, then triumphantly held up several strands of small, electrical black wires.

Sophia and the rest of the women stared in confusion.

"Okay," Sophia finally said slowly, not understanding. "What am I looking at here?"

"Wires," I said. "I'm no expert, but I'd be willing to bet that these hairclips are all actually tiny listening devices. Someone convinced you to sell them so that people here would buy them, and then the person who sold them to you would have little microphones all over town to eavesdrop on conversations."

Sophia turned pale. "Really? These clips are rigged?"

I nodded. "I think so." I held the wires right in front of my eyes to look at them. I couldn't tell exactly what all of the wires were supposed to do, but I knew that they weren't intended to hold hair in place.

"Well," Rose said, almost reverently. "That's some James Bond stuff right there."

I nodded, then turned my attention back to Sophia. "Listen, what can you tell me about the person who sold you these clips?"

The color continued to drain from Sophia's face. "I couldn't tell you that much. Some woman came in offering me a great deal on these hairclips. She said they were handmade and contained real crystals, but that due to overproduction, she needed to sell them at a discount. She even had a certificate to prove that the crystals were real. I couldn't pass up a deal like that. It was so cheap to buy all of them, and they were so beautiful that I knew the women in Sunshine Springs would love them. They've sold well, so at least half the women in Sunshine Springs have the clips now." Sophia put her face in her hands. "I can't believe this. I wasn't meaning to sell something to everyone that would open them up to an eavesdropper. Do you think this person has something to do with Tom's murder?"

"Possibly," I said. "But it's not your fault, Sophia. How were you supposed to know that the clips were rigged?"

All across the room, women were reaching up to pull the hairclips out of their hair, staring at them as though they'd suddenly been told that the clips were radioactive. Even Grams, who normally took everything in stride, was looking a little pale.

I had to get this information to Mitch, and fast. But first, I wanted to see whether Sophia knew anything else. Mitch would probably appreciate any information I could give him. I hoped he would understand that I hadn't been trying to go back on my word to stay out of this case. It's just that this clue had practically fallen into my lap.

Sophia was shaking her head slowly. "I can't remember much. I was so enamored with the clips that I didn't pay much attention to the woman. She was short, if I remember right. She had dirty blonde hair that was cropped to her chin, and I think she said her name was Janessa Fletcher.

"That's a bit of an unusual name," I said. "Maybe if I look online, something about her will come up."

I pulled out my phone and quickly entered the name "Janessa

Fletcher" into my internet browser. The first hit that came up was the Facebook profile of a woman by that name. The woman had cropped, dirty blonde hair just as Sophia had mentioned, and her location was listed as Lilac Canyon—the next town over.

I felt my heart dropping to my feet. I had a feeling that I'd just found the murderer. I wasn't sure exactly who this woman was, why she would have wanted to kill Tom, or why she was so curious to learn all of Sunshine Springs' secrets. But one thing I knew for sure: I wouldn't be able to get this information to Mitch fast enough.

I tried to remain calm as I went back to the manicure chair to gather up my purse and keys. My rental car still hadn't arrived at the salon, so I needed to borrow Grams' car again.

"Grams? Is it alright if I run a quick errand with your car?"

Grams nodded, still looking pale. She didn't even bother telling me that I better not be sleuthing. She was probably too shocked by the knowledge that all of her conversations over the last several days had been potentially transmitted to some stranger.

I walked back over to the display of hairclips and picked up the whole thing. "I need to borrow these, if you don't mind," I said to Sophia.

Sophia nodded. "Please, take them. I don't want them anymore. I feel so violated!"

I nodded back at her, and turned toward the front door. I didn't want to actually say that I was going to see Mitch. For all I knew, the hairclips were broadcasting right now, and this Janessa Fletcher character was eagerly listening in to see what I was going to do next. I didn't want to tip her off that I was going to see Mitch, so I kept my mouth shut about it.

But Rose couldn't help being nosy. "Where are you going with the clips?" she asked.

Everyone leaned forward eagerly, waiting to hear the answer.

"I'm just going to run an important errand," I said, trying to keep my voice calm. "I'll make sure these clips are stashed away somewhere that no more secrets will be getting out through them."

With that, I rushed out the front door before anyone could ask any more questions. I only hoped that the murderer wouldn't be smart enough to realize I was going to Mitch—or, at least, that they wouldn't be close enough to intercept me before I got there.

With chills racing down my spine, I floored the accelerator on Grams' car and headed toward the Sunshine Springs Police Station.

CHAPTER TWENTY-TWO

I pulled into the police station parking lot far too fast, my heart pounding with excitement as I swerved into a parking spot and then quickly made my way inside. Sprinkles ran in behind me, refusing to wait calmly outside like he usually did. The receptionist looked up at us both, startled.

"Izzy? Is everything all right?"

"Hold these," I said in response, and threw the bundle of hairclips down onto her desk. Then, without another word, I ran back to Mitch's office. The door was closed, so I pounded on it, hoping he was in there. I hadn't wanted to have the receptionist call him, because I was afraid that if whoever was behind the hairclips was eavesdropping that they would realize I was at the police station and would try to make a run for it.

A moment later, the door to Mitch's office opened. Mitch was grumbling as he opened the door. "What in the world is all this commotion about? This better be something important, and—"

When he saw me, and saw the expression on my face, he stopped short. "What's wrong?"

Instead of answering I put a finger to my lips to warn him to be quiet. Then I quickly ran past him into his office and grabbed the hairclip that had been sitting on his bookshelf earlier that day. I darted back into the hallway and threw the hairclip down the hall with all my might before pulling Mitch back into his office and slamming the door shut. Mitch looked at me like he thought that this time I really had lost my mind.

"What in the world are you doing? You can't just throw that hairclip down the hallway! That's evidence!"

"Just hear me out," I said. As quickly as I could, I told him everything that I'd just learned at Sophia's Snips. Mitch listened, skeptically at first. But his face gradually grew more and more concerned. A look of horror crossed his face when he realized that I was serious. He ran back into the hallway and picked up the hairclip I'd thrown out there so that no one would overhear me talking to him. He pulled the clip out of its clear, plastic evidence bag and put the clip on his desk. Then he grabbed the blunt end of his revolver and smashed it—just as I had smashed one back at Sophia's with her phone.

And just like the hairclip I'd smashed at Sophia's, this one was filled with small wires. Mitch stared down at it for several moments in disbelief, then calmly picked up his phone and called one of his officers.

"Smith? I've got some evidence that we're going to need to take a second look at. Can you send someone over to pick it up? I'll leave it at the reception desk."

Once Mitch had finished speaking with his officer, he turned back and frowned at me. "This is a big development in the case, and I'm glad you figured this out. But what happened to not sleuthing anymore? You promised me!"

He didn't actually look angry. The expression on his face was more of disappointment than anything, and I was surprised at how much that hurt me. I definitely didn't want to disappoint him.

"I wasn't trying to sleuth, I swear. I was just sitting there, minding my own business and trying to get my nails done. But then Sophia and one of the ladies in the salon said something that made me realize that these hairclips might be more sinister than we realized. I smashed one open and found the wires. I guess I can't be sure until somebody who knows about this sort of thing examines the clips, but it sure seems to me like they're being used to spy on Sunshine Springs residents. And since we found them at the crime scene, perhaps they're all tied in with whoever murdered Tom."

The disappointment on Mitch's face faded as he considered all of this. "I see. I guess I can't be too surprised that you found out something by accident while at Sophia's salon. Sometimes I think I should just spend my days there and my detective work would all get done a lot faster. In fact, I suppose I should go there now and talk to Sophia about this. She's not going to be thrilled about my asking her for another statement, although she will probably be happy to know that I'm directing my suspicions somewhere besides her—not that I ever really thought she could be responsible. But it sounds like whoever sold her those hairclips might be the murderer we're looking for."

"I definitely think that the hairclip seller is behind this," I agreed. "But I don't think you should go talk to Sophia now. I think you should try to find the person who sold her the clips first. Sophia already gave me her name and told me as much as she could about her. If we waste more time talking to Sophia, we give our suspect time to get away. I don't know how much they heard of what I said to Sophia at the hair salon, but it might have been enough for them to get suspicious and try to run."

Mitch scratched his chin as he considered this, and I could tell that he was unsure of what to do.

"I don't want to tell you how to do your job," I said quickly. "Honest, I don't. But I do think that maybe you should consider going after this Janessa Fletcher girl directly to try to catch her before she fully realizes that we're onto her."

I half expected Mitch to be irritated with me for trying to tell him how to do his job. But he considered my comments thoughtfully and nodded. "You're probably right. I'll call the sheriff over in Lilac Canyon and see if he's heard of this girl."

I stood patiently by while Mitch made the phone call. I could hardly believe that he was letting me stay for this. I'd expected him to kick me out, but he seemed to be too caught up in the excitement of everything that was going on to be worried about kicking me out. In fact, he even put the phone on speaker, which allowed me to listen in on the whole conversation. I wasn't sure whether he did that for my benefit, or whether he normally took his calls on speakerphone so that he wouldn't have to hold the receiver. But either way, I could hardly contain my excitement as I listened in.

"Joe? It's Mitch over in Sunshine Springs. How are you?"

"Mitch! Good to hear from you. I'm great. How are you holding up?"

"I'm alright. But listen, we have a bit of a situation over here."

Mitch quickly explained about the hairclips, and about how Sophia had said a woman named Janessa Fletcher from Lilac Canyon had sold them to her. When he was done, he asked, "Do you happen to know this Janessa Fletcher girl?"

"Yes, I know her," the Lilac Canyon Sheriff replied. "She's been a resident of Lilac Canyon her whole life."

"And?" Mitch asked. "Is she a troublemaker? Does it make sense to you that she would be involved in this sort of thing?"

The other sheriff paused for a moment before speaking. "Well, that's an interesting question. She's actually always been a pretty decent person, but lately, she has been causing a bit of trouble. It all started when she started hanging out with this girl Ruby. Maybe you know her, in fact. Ruby Phillips? I think she recently moved to your town."

I looked at Mitch with wide eyes, and he raised an eyebrow at me.

"Ruby?" he said into the phone. "Yeah I know her. She moved here to work at one of our local cafés, but as far as I know she hasn't caused any trouble here."

The other sheriff snorted. "Well, just you wait. Ruby is bound to stir things up eventually. She was nothing but a bad influence on Janessa."

"Hmm," Mitch said. "I'll keep an eye out for Ruby. But in the meantime, do you think you could see if you could bring Janessa in for questioning? I'm happy to drive out to Lilac Canyon to talk to her if you can get her down to your station there."

"Sure thing," the other sheriff said. "I'll bring her in." There was a short pause, and then the other sheriff sighed. "I have to say that this is quite disappointing. Janessa's been stirring things up a bit lately, but I am shocked to hear that she's been eavesdropping and possibly involved in a murder case. I don't understand how she could fall so far so fast. But I guess these things have a way of surprising you."

"Ain't that the truth," Mitch said sadly. "Thanks for all your help. I'll head down to Lilac Canyon as soon as you get Janessa at the station."

"Sure thing. I'll keep you posted."

Mitch ended the call and ran his fingers through his hair before cracking his knuckles. For a few moments, we were both silent. Then, Mitch stood up. "Well, I guess, there's nothing to do now except wait for the Lilac Canyon Sheriff to call me back. What are you going to do? Head to the salon and finish your manicure?"

I glanced down at Sprinkles, whose toenails were already painted. I wasn't sure I wanted to go back to the salon now, but before I could make up my mind and tell Mitch what I was going to do, Mitch's phone rang with a call from the reception desk.

"What's up?" Mitch asked the receptionist after hitting the speaker button to take the call.

"I'm really sorry to bother you," the receptionist said, sounding quite frustrated. "But there's a girl out here insisting on talking to you. She said it's important and can't wait."

"Okay," Mitch said slowly. "Did she give her name?"

"Yes, Janessa Fletcher. I don't think she's a local, but she said she needs to talk to you and that it's urgent."

Mitch and I looked at each other, both of our eyes widening in shock.

"Janessa Fletcher?" Mitch choked out, unable to believe it.

"Yes. You know her? Should I send her back?"

"Yes," Mitch said, already starting toward the door. "Bring her to Interview Room A right away. I definitely want to talk to her."

CHAPTER TWENTY-THREE

When Mitch and I entered the interview room, Janessa was already sitting there, and she was a blubbering mess. When we walked in, she looked up and started sobbing even harder.

"Please, can you help me?" she pleaded.

"We'll certainly do our best," Mitch said. "Why don't you take a few deep breaths and tell me what's going on."

Janessa nodded and did as Mitch said, although I wasn't sure how much good the deep breaths were doing her. She still looked quite distraught.

Mitch remained patient, letting her breathe for a few moments without interrupting her. I kept expecting him to realize I was there and boot me out of the interview room, but he never did. If he noticed or cared that Sprinkles and I were in there, he never said anything. Sprinkles and I were still sitting there when Janessa finally calmed down enough to talk.

"I need your help. I'm in over my head and I don't know who to go to." Her lower lip trembled and she looked like she might start sobbing again.

Mitch spoke in a calm, soothing voice. "We'll do everything we can to help you, and you're safe here. Why don't you just tell me what's going on?"

I wondered if he was thinking the same thing that I was: this girl certainly did not look like a bloodthirsty murderer. But perhaps she was feeling remorseful and didn't know how to confess. I squirmed impatiently as she continued to sob more than speak. Finally, though, she managed to get out what she wanted to say.

"There's a woman in your town who is trying to steal from your citizens. She's gathering information in order to conduct a huge identity theft scheme."

Mitch raised an eyebrow. "Okay," he said encouragingly. "And what can you tell us about this scheme?"

"This woman has been gathering information on all sorts of things—bank account numbers, mother's maiden names, even things like favorite colors or foods, or anything else that might be used as passwords. She's trying to steal records that would have Social Security numbers, and she's planning to wipe out the savings of as many people as possible in Sunshine Springs."

Here, Janessa paused for a moment, then took a deep breath and said. "I know all of this because she's been forcing me to help her set up the surveillance audio. I borrowed money from her as a personal loan about a year ago, but I fell on hard times and couldn't repay her. She said that unless I helped her, she'd repossess my car, which I'd put up as collateral for the loan. I can't afford to lose my car, or I'll lose my job. Then things will get worse from there. I agreed to help her even though I didn't feel good about the audio surveillance, because I didn't see what choice I really had. At first, I tried to tell myself that she was just playing around and it wasn't going to be anything serious. But then, she started asking me for more and more help in getting these surveillance devices out."

"How did she get them out?" Mitch asked, even though we both already knew. I figured he just wanted confirmation.

"She forced me to go sell them super cheap to a hairdresser here in town so that the hair dresser would sell the hairclips to Sunshine Springs residents. Then the audio devices would be all over town. That's when I really got suspicious and started trying to figure out what she was doing. I don't know exactly how deep all of this goes, but I know that I don't even know the half of it. Ruby found out that I knew about her plans, and started threatening me even worse. Maybe this sounds crazy, but I'm starting to get worried for my life. She's said all sorts of things that implied she would kill me if I didn't cooperate. I don't know if she would actually go through with it, but I'm afraid to take any more chances. Please, can you help me?"

I looked over at Mitch, and my jaw dropped. He looked just as shocked as me. Slowly, he turned back to look at Janessa.

"Wait a minute. Did you just say Ruby? Ruby Phillips?"

Janessa looked up from her sobbing in surprise. "Yes, she's the one behind all of this. You know her?"

Mitch looked back at me, and I felt a slow feeling of horror creeping over me.

"It's Ruby," I said in a voice barely louder than a whisper. "She's behind the audio surveillance, and she killed Tom for some reason. He must have gotten tangled up in this."

Mitch sprang to his feet. "Janessa, stay here for now. You'll be safe in the police station, and we might need to ask you some questions later. If you need anything, the receptionist out front can get it for you. Just don't leave the police station, and you won't get hurt." Then he looked over at me. "You, come on. Let's roll."

I stood in confusion. "Where are we going?"

"To Ruby's house. I just hope that she hasn't realized yet that we know about her, and that we're not too late to catch her."

"You want me to come with you? But I thought you wanted me to stay out of this case?"

Mitch shook his head at me. "I think it's a little too late now for you to stay out of it. It looks like your employee is the one behind all of this. I might need your help in finding her if she's not at home, or even just in talking to her if she is at home. Don't worry. You'll be safe with me. Now let's go."

He rushed out of the room without another word. I looked at Sprinkles, shrugged, and followed Mitch with Sprinkles right behind me. I jumped into the passenger seat of Mitch's patrol car, and Sprinkles jumped into the backseat.

Mitch started speeding down the road, sirens and lights blazing, and Sprinkles started barking excitedly. This must have been quite exciting for him.

It was exciting for me, too, but I wasn't sure if the excitement was a good thing. My heart pounded as Mitch pulled onto the road.

"Do you know where Ruby lives?" he asked me. "Or should I call one of my officers to give me that info?"

"I know," I said. "At least, if the address she put on her employment application was correct, then I know. I remember because I thought it was a bit of an expensive area for someone working at a pie shop."

I rattled off the address, and Mitch looked at me in surprise.

"Really? That *is* quite an expensive area for someone who works at a pie shop. I hope it's the right address."

I shrugged. "Maybe Ruby has a lot more money than someone who just works at a pie shop. It certainly sounds like she's been keeping up a racket on the side."

"Only one way to find out," Mitch said, and floored the accelerator toward the address I'd given him.

CHAPTER TWENTY-FOUR

Less than ten minutes later, we were pulling in front of the house that Ruby supposedly lived at. I peered out the window, trying to see if I recognized her car, but the driveway was empty. If she did live here, and she was home, her car must be in the garage right now.

"Stay here," Mitch ordered. "I'm going in."

But as he reached for his door handle, I saw the front door of the house open. Ruby rushed out and took off running.

"There she is!" I shrieked. "That's her! She's making a run for it!"

Mitch moved faster than I'd ever seen him move before. He practically launched himself out of the car and sprinted across the grass toward Ruby.

"Ruby Phillips, you're under arrest for the murder of Tom Schmidt!"

Ruby shrieked and tried to keep running, but it was no use. She couldn't outrun Mitch, and in less than half a minute he'd caught up to her. He began wrangling her wrists into handcuffs, with her fighting him the whole time. She couldn't match his strength, though, and a few moments later, Mitch had her fully restrained. He spun her around so he could look her in the eye, then shook his head at her in disgust. "Ruby Phillips, you're under arrest. You have the right to remain silent…"

His voice was drowned out as more cop cars started approaching, their sirens still blaring. Ruby looked up and gave me a wounded look, as though I had somehow betrayed her. Feeling disgusted, I looked away. I turned to the backseat to look at Sprinkles, who was watching the scene in front of him quite alertly.

"Well, Sprinkles," I said ruefully. "I guess we helped solve this case as well. I can't seem to stay out of things no matter how hard I try."

A sharp rap at my window startled me, and I turned around quickly, thinking it was one of the officers who had just arrived on the scene. To my shock, I saw Molly and Scott standing beside the car. I threw the door open quickly and shook my head at Molly. "This isn't what you think. I can explain! I wasn't trying to get involved in another case."

Then I paused and frowned at her. "Come to think of it, what are *you* doing here?"

Molly's eyes were wide, and she looked back and forth between me and the chaos unfolding in front of us. Ruby was screaming louder than ever, and Mitch's officers that had just arrived were trying to help keep her calm.

Molly looked back at me. "Ruby is the murderer?"

I nodded. "It would appear that way."

Scott shook his head. "Well, I'll be. Molly and I were just strolling through the neighborhood, spending our lunch breaks looking at dream houses that we'll probably never be able to afford. We heard all the noise and rushed over to this street to see what was going on. Imagine our shock when we saw you sitting here."

"I can explain," I said again. "But it's a long story."

"I want to hear everything," Molly said eagerly. "But first, let's not miss a chance for another crime scene selfie."

I groaned. "Really? You're going to make me do that again?"

Molly grinned at me. "Of course. I can't miss the chance to add to my collection of selfies with arrested murderers in the background."

She pulled her cell phone out, pulled me out of the car, and wrapped her arm around my shoulders.

"Say cheese," she said as she held the phone up.

"Cheese," I said in an exaggerated tone.

Molly ignored my annoyed attitude and snapped a few shots. "Perfect. You'll be seeing those online later today."

I rolled my eyes at her again, but I couldn't truly be upset. Not when it looked like another murder case had been solved, and I would finally feel safe walking the streets of Sunshine Springs once again. I was about to start explaining things to Molly, but then Mitch called me over.

"I'll catch up with you guys in a bit," I said. "Let me go see what Mitch wants. Hopefully he's going to tell me that they found hard evidence that Ruby is guilty."

I crossed my fingers as I walked over to Mitch, praying that he would indeed be able to say for sure that Ruby was the murderer. I was ready for this case to be completely closed and for life to go back to normal.

As I jogged up to Mitch, Ruby spat in my face. "How could you betray me like this," she screeched. "After all the hard work I've done for you!"

I stared at her in disbelief.

"Are you kidding me?" I asked. "I've paid you well for all your hard work. And no matter how hard you've worked at the café, that doesn't give you the right to kill people or steal from the citizens of Sunshine Springs."

"And it looks like she was indeed killing and stealing," one of Mitch's officers said as he approached us and overheard my comment. We all turned to look at him, and saw that he was holding several bags of evidence. "Looks like we found everything we need."

The officer held up the first of the plastic bags. "These scissors look like they came from Sophia's salon. They must be an extra pair Ruby stole when she stole the scissors that she actually used to put the gash on the back of Tom's head." The officer held up another bag, this one full of cash. "We found piles of cash, listening devices, and a ton of notes on sensitive information from people in Sunshine Springs. It looks like you have indeed found your criminal."

"You hear that, Ruby?" Mitch asked. "We've got all the evidence we need. There's no sense in trying to deny things further. You're being accused of murder, among other things. If you want to make it easier on yourself, I suggest talking and cooperating. The easier you make this, the better chance you have of getting the best possible deal you can in court."

Ruby looked stricken, and for a moment I thought she was going to continue to deny everything. But then, she seemed to completely break down. "This all happened because Tom couldn't keep his nose out of places it didn't belong!"

And that's when I realized exactly what was going on.

"Tom figured out what you are doing, didn't he?" I said. "He must have threatened to go to the cops, and you took him out because of that."

Ruby looked at me and sneered. "Yeah, Tom was a lowlife. He wanted a cut of whatever money I was making, but I wasn't about to share. He threatened to tell the cops if I didn't pull him into it, so I made sure that he would never tell anyone anything about what I was doing."

Even though Ruby had all but confessed at this point, I couldn't keep my eyes from widening when she said this. "It was you, wasn't it? You changed the clues on the scavenger hunt. Belinda must have told you everything. She considered you her best friend, and you betrayed her trust. You let her explain the whole scavenger hunt to you, and then you carefully changed the clues so that Tom would be exactly where you wanted him to be at exactly the right time."

Ruby let out a maniacal sounding laugh. "Yes, it was me that changed the clues. Belinda was so dumb. She told me everything, and trusted me even though she didn't really know me. I made sure Tom would be at the lemon grove. Then I called Belinda and pretended to be someone warning her that Tom was in danger. I wanted her out there right around the time of the murder so that she would look guilty. Unfortunately, she took a little longer to get out there than I thought she would, so the timing wasn't perfect. But it was still good enough for people to question whether she had already been out there and had murdered Tom. Later, I pretended I didn't know about the changed clues, just to throw you off further and make sure you weren't at all suspicious that I was involved."

I wrinkled my nose at her in disgust. "And what about Sophia? Did you call her to come out to the murder scene, too?"

Ruby nodded, apparently willing to let the whole story spill out now that she was on a roll. "I knew that Sophia was having trouble with Tom over some business dealings gone bad. I called her, pretending to be someone who said they could meet with her and Tom to help negotiate a solution between them. Sophia was so desperate that she never really questioned how odd that was. I made sure she drove by the lemon grove at just about the time that the murder happened. She saw Tom's car there and recognized it, so she got out to investigate. She was the first one to find the body, and was predictably distraught. Of course, I wasn't counting on you and your Grams driving by at that exact moment. That really put a wrench in my plans."

"Yeah," Mitch said, his voice filling with pride. "It sure put a wrench in your plans when Sunshine Springs' finest amateur sleuth was on your trail, didn't it?"

I looked over at Mitch, surprised by the praise. He saw the surprise in my face and merely winked at me. I smiled at him, figuring that even though he didn't like it when I played detective, he was loyal enough to defend me when someone else from the outside was disparaging me.

Then, suddenly, another realization hit me, and I turned to look at Ruby again. "Wait a minute. The slow sales that afternoon were because you had actually closed the pie shop, weren't they? You never told me you closed, because you wanted me to think that the shop had been open and you'd been there all day working. You thought it gave you a good alibi, and that I would never think to suspect you." My mind kept racing as I remembered another day of slow sales. "And you closed the afternoon that the lemon grove burned, didn't you? That was you!"

Ruby shrugged. "You're too nice for your own good, Izzy. I knew you saw the slow sales, but I knew you wouldn't say anything, because you'd figure I was having a hard time settling in as a new employee."

"Why did you burn the lemon grove?" Mitch asked. "What evidence were you worried about?"

Ruby rolled her eyes. "I wasn't worried about evidence. I actually didn't know when I went to burn the grove that you had already been planning to go back and comb for more evidence. I was just trying to get Izzy out there. I knew that if she heard that the lemon grove was burning, she wouldn't be able to resist going to look. I had planted a hairclip out there so I could hear and make sure I knew when she left. I wanted her out on those country roads by herself in the dark."

My stomach flip-flopped, and I felt sick. "It was you that ran me off the road."

Ruby shrugged, not looking even the least bit remorseful. "You were getting too nosy, and I was afraid you were going to figure everything out. Unfortunately, you refused to die, and I realized I'd have to find another way to take you out. But in the meantime, I had to continue to distract you and make you think it wasn't me, so I broke into the pie shop."

Mitch frowned. "Why would you break in when you worked there and had a key..."

"That's exactly it," I said to Mitch. "She figured that since she could get into the pie shop without actually breaking in, that no one would suspect that she was the burglar. That's why nothing was missing. The point wasn't to take anything. The point was just to throw me off her trail."

Ruby crossed her arms and glared at me. "This all would have worked out perfectly if it wasn't for you. You can never just mind your own business, can you?"

I glared at her. "Sunshine Springs is my home now, and what happens here is my business. You killed a man who lived here. He may not have been everyone's favorite, but he didn't deserve to die. Not only that, but you've also left Belinda, one of our longtime Sunshine Springs residents, completely heartbroken. You should be ashamed of yourself."

Ruby threw back her head and laughed. "*I* should be ashamed of myself? Tom should have been ashamed of himself. That guy was such a fraud. He was always just trying to cheat people out of their money. You've already seen that Sophia was dumb enough to fall for his schemes. But not only that, he was also a sleaze who made Belinda believe he cared about her. He was just having a little bit of fun with her and never intended for anything between them to be long term. In fact, he tried to come onto me, and told me he'd keep things quiet about my little operations if I slept with him. But he messed with the wrong girl when he tried to blackmail me. He'll never blackmail anyone ever again."

Ruby crossed her arms and stuck her chin out triumphantly, apparently still not feeling much remorse over the fact that she'd actually killed someone.

"Alright, that's enough," Mitch said, then turned to one of his officers. "Smith, get this woman down to the station and get an official statement from her. She's got quite a bit of explaining to do, and I have a feeling that the judge in her case isn't going to be impressed with her explanations."

Smith dragged Ruby away, and Mitch turned to look at me with a searching gaze. "Are you alright? Really? That must be quite a lot to take in."

I shrugged. "I'm definitely shocked by all of it, but I'm alright. At least I know now that Tom's murderer is caught and I'll be safe. Besides, it feels good to know that it wasn't Belinda or Sophia. I really couldn't bring myself to think that either of them would do something so awful."

"Neither could I," Mitch said. "Although, it was hard to figure out who else could have possibly done it. I really owe you one, Izzy. You know you drive me crazy when you insist on chasing down clues, but I have to admit you're pretty darn good at it."

I beamed. "Thanks, but you're right. It is a bit dangerous. This last case has really made that hit home for me. I think I'd be happy if things settled down for a while."

Mitch reached over and gave my shoulder an affectionate squeeze. "I think they will, and you definitely deserve a break. In fact, why don't I drive you back to Sophia's salon, and you can finish that manicure you started this morning?"

Sprinkles looked up at me and barked in agreement, and I laughed. "You know what, I think I will. I'm a little jealous of Sprinkles' beautiful turquoise nails."

To make everything even better than it already was, Molly agreed to head to the salon with me, saying she could use a manicure as well. Scott bowed out and told us to have fun, and I felt like everything was right with the world again. I was safe, and it was clear that Molly's relationship with Scott wasn't going to ruin our friendship. She was happy, I was happy, and I had a feeling that Sophia was going to be *very* happy when I brought her the news that she'd been officially cleared of murder.

Today had been a wonderful day to be a citizen of Sunshine Springs.

CHAPTER TWENTY-FIVE

One week later, I held a small party after hours at the Drunken Pie Café. I wanted to thank everyone who had been there for me during Tom's murder case, so I invited Mitch, Theo, Scott, and Molly. Grams and Sprinkles were there too, of course. Grams had been a godsend when I needed a place to stay after the wreck, and I couldn't thank Sprinkles enough for his part in rescuing me from my wrecked car. I invited Belinda and Sophia as well. I wanted them to know that I understood that it had been hard to go through what they'd been through. I myself had once been falsely accused of murder, and I knew it was a stressful time.

Besides, I needed an excuse to throw a party. I'd been baking like crazy every night, trying out recipes for potential holiday menus. I needed a group of friends to test the recipes and give me their honest opinion. In addition to the spiked Christmas pie, I was considering a cranberry vodka crumble, a peppermint schnapps chocolate cream pie, and an eggnog bourbon pie. These would be additions to my normal menu that would only be available during the holiday season, and I could hardly wait to see what my friends thought of them.

I set up the pies buffet style, and encouraged everyone to try as many different ones as they wanted. I also set out bottles of wine from Theo's winery. I always served his wine in my pie shop, but I thought that his pinots paired especially well with the holiday flavors.

Soon, everyone had slices of pie in front of them, and they were sitting around at the café tables munching and talking happily.

"The cranberry vodka crumble is my favorite," Grams said. "The eggnog bourbon pie is a close second, but my number one vote goes to the cranberry pie. It has the best boozy flavor of all of them."

I laughed. "You sure know what you like in a pie."

"I sure do," Grams said. "And Sprinkles does, too. He likes the cranberry vodka crumble the best as well."

"Grams!" I groaned. "You know Sprinkles isn't supposed to be eating boozy pie."

"He's not?" Grams said in an overly innocent voice.

I just rolled my eyes at her. She knew very well that I didn't like giving Sprinkles boozy pie, even though most of the alcohol was cooked out when the pies baked. But Grams ignored me and fed Sprinkles boozy pie all the time, anyway. I had given up on that battle, realizing that she was going to do what she wanted to do no matter what I said. So far, Sprinkles seemed to be surviving all the extra pie he got from her.

"The peppermint schnapps pie is my favorite," Belinda piped in. "Although, I won't be around this holiday season to enjoy it."

The room fell silent, and everyone turned to look at Belinda.

"What do you mean?" I asked.

Belinda took a deep breath, then looked around with a sad smile on her face. "I've decided to move to San Francisco. Sunshine Springs has been a great home for me for my whole life, but now that Frank and I have split up and then Tom was killed here, there are just too many sad memories for me. I think it would be good if I had a fresh start somewhere new."

I nodded sympathetically. "I certainly understand the need for a fresh start. We'll be sad to see you go, but I wish you all the best in your new adventures."

Around the room, everyone murmured echoes of that sentiment. Belinda looked relieved, as though she'd been afraid to tell everyone her plans. I couldn't say I blamed her. She'd been through a lot here in the last month or two, and it would probably be easier for her to move forward without all that baggage hanging off of her.

"You have to come get one last haircut from me before you leave, dear," Sophia said to Belinda. Then, Sophia turned to me and said, "And you, Izzy. You get free haircuts for life at my salon."

I gasped. "Don't be ridiculous, Sophia. That's generous of you to offer, but I didn't do anything to deserve that big of a gift."

But Sophia was insistent. "You helped clear my name of murder. I think that deserves a huge reward, so I'm giving it to you: free haircuts for life."

I wanted to protest again, especially since I knew Sophia had been having financial troubles. But Sophia seemed to have anticipated that I would say this, because she shook her head at me. "Besides, I can afford to give free haircuts now. It turns out that quite a few of the transactions Tom did with me were illegal, and the court set them aside. The money I paid him was returned to me when his estate was probated. My bank account is no longer empty, and I've learned my lesson: no more crazy real estate deals for me."

Molly reached over and patted Sophia's hand. "I'm so glad everything worked out for you. And don't worry about your reputation in the community. Everyone knows that we all make mistakes, and no one thinks less of you for going over a few bumps in the road."

Sophia looked gratefully back at Molly, and I caught Scott beaming over at Molly. He slung his arm around her, and planted a kiss on her cheek.

I had to admit that, strange as it was to see them together, they just fit. I couldn't believe I'd never seen it before, but Molly's sass and Scott's humor blended well.

At that moment, there was a knock at the front door of my café. I looked over to see Alice, the owner of another café in town known as the Morning Brew Café. She poked her head in and looked around the room with a bit of embarrassment turning her cheeks pink.

"I'm sorry, Izzy. I didn't realize that you had guests here. I was just hoping to catch you before you went home. I know that you've been through a lot in the last few weeks, and I thought maybe you could use a little boost. I brought you a care package."

She held out a small basket to me, and I saw that it was filled with freshly baked muffins from her café, as well as a bag of her coffee that she roasted in-house.

I took the basket from her and set it on a table, then pulled her into a quick hug.

"Thank you so much. That was so thoughtful of you. Please, since you're here, stay and have some pie. I'm testing out my holiday menu, and I'd love to hear your thoughts."

Alice groaned. "Okay, but only if you promise to come help me test out my holiday menu next week in return. I'm finalizing it right now."

My smile widened. "Of course. I'm not going to pass up the chance to eat Christmas muffins from your café."

Alice loaded up her plate and settled into a conversation with Grams. I noticed that she looked over at Scott and Molly with a bit of a longing, jealous look, and I wondered if Alice wished to find love as well. She was a kind, smart woman, and a savvy business owner. It was a wonder to me that she hadn't settled down yet, but, then again, neither had I. Just because someone was a good catch didn't mean they'd found the right person to catch them yet.

As the pie tasting wound down, Mitch stood and prepared to leave.

He walked over and gave me a thumbs up. "If you want my opinion, I still think the Christmas spiked pie is the best. But they're all good. You've got a winning menu there, and I can't wait to stop by the café every day in December to get fat on your Christmas pie."

I laughed. "I don't think you'll ever get fat. You like working out too much for that."

Mitch shrugged. "We'll see. If I do get fat, I'm blaming you and your pie. It's too hard to resist."

He gave me a wink and then pulled me into a big bear hug. "I'm just glad you're safe. Try to stay out of trouble now, eh?"

I smiled as I smelled the familiar scent of his aftershave. He really was a good guy, but I still felt that he fit me better as a friend than a boyfriend.

As he walked out, Molly caught my eye and raised an eyebrow, and I knew she was asking whether there had been something more to the hug than friendliness. I would have to set her straight later, and tell her that there was nothing between Mitch and me. At least, there was nothing between us as far as I was concerned. Mitch still acted as determined as ever to let me know he was available, but I wasn't going to fall for his charms—especially not now, with my life as busy as it was. Since Ruby was obviously gone from the café, I was once again on the hunt for an employee. Until I found one, I'd be busy running things by myself as I had been for most of my café's short existence.

I started to clear plates from the table, and I saw my friends standing up to help. But before I could even wave them off and tell them not to worry about cleaning up, there was another sharp rap at my door. I looked up, surprised to see that Moe, who owned a souvenir shop next door, was rushing in and waving his hands excitedly.

"Everyone! Come quick! I just heard that Big Al Martel is coming to town and stopped at the ice-cream parlor. You guys want to see? I can't believe there's a celebrity in our town!"

"What?" Grams exclaimed. "I've never seen a celebrity in person. Let's go!" She ran out of the restaurant following Moe, and everyone else ran after her. Well, everyone except Sprinkles and Theo. Sprinkles was lying contentedly on the ground, happy with his sugar rush from all the pie he'd eaten and completely unimpressed with the idea of seeing a celebrity. I myself wasn't that excited about seeing Big Al Martel. I'd actually seen him in San Francisco a few times, and didn't find it that exciting to just catch a glimpse of someone famous. Apparently, Theo didn't find it exciting either, because he held back as well.

I raised an eyebrow at him. "Don't want to see Big Al Martel?"

He shrugged, and gave me one of his winning smiles. "I'd rather see you."

I laughed, and couldn't help teasing him a bit. "What's the matter? A little bit threatened by the hug Mitch gave me?"

"Should I be?" he asked in a completely serious tone of voice.

I smiled kindly at him. "No, because I'm not interested in dating either of you. You know that. We've been over this."

Theo shrugged. "You can't blame me for trying again and again, can you? Not when you're the spunkiest, most beautiful woman I've ever met."

My cheeks heated up at the praise, but I forced myself to act natural. "Look, Theo. Things are finally settling down here. My café is doing well, and even though I just lost my employee, I think I'm settling into a groove here. I need to focus on work, and I need to spend some time getting ready for the fall festival. Not only am I thinking of entering Sprinkles in the dog show, but I'm also planning to have a booth selling pie. It's a busy time, and I'm just not interested in a relationship right now."

"I was afraid of that," Theo said. "I always get some version of that story from you, but I'll keep asking you until one day you change your mind."

He winked at me, and I shrugged. "As long as you know that you might be asking for a very, very long time."

"That's okay. You're the kind of person who's worth the wait. But in the meantime, can I at least promise to buy you a candy-coated apple at the fall festival?"

I smiled. "I guess I could allow that. Relaxing at a fall festival with a delicious candy-coated apple sounds like just the thing I need after all the excitement of Tom's murder case."

Theo laughed. "Don't worry. I'm sure there'll be more excitement coming. There always is with you."

I shook my head no emphatically. "Not anymore. I promised Mitch I'd give up my sleuthing ways. I'm pretty sure I've had all the excitement I'm going to have for a long, long time."

Theo just shrugged at me again, and went to start cleaning up the remaining pie. "We'll see," he said. "I'm not sure you know how to live life any other way than full of excitement."

To be honest, I wasn't sure, either. I was just glad that, for now, the excitement had ended with a murderer being caught—and that the streets of Sunshine Springs were safe once again.

ABOUT THE AUTHOR

Diana DuMont lives and writes in Northern California. When she's not reading or dreaming up her latest mystery plot, she can usually be found hiking in the nearby redwood forests. You can connect with her at www.dianadumont.com.